◄ T H E   I C E   Q U E E N ►

"Electrifying. . . . In Alice Hoffman's best novel since *Practical Magic* bewitched readers in 1995, a woman haunted by a tragic childhood wish finds her life transformed by a shocking lightning strike. . . . It's within the narrator's passionate affair that Hoffman's prose conveys an eroticism hinted in earlier books but never explored before with such intensity. . . . A poignant denouement provides a wonderful, magical catharsis. . . . Hoffman explores the consequences of both magic and lightning with luminous clarity. It is a stunning feat."   — Melissa Mia Hall, *Chicago Sun-Times*

"*The Ice Queen* is an adult fairy tale that warps the boundaries of everyday existence. Hoffman's heroine, a librarian with pale skin, dark hair, and a heart of ice (vaguely reminiscent of Snow White), embarks on a sensual and emotional journey."
  — Ashley Simpson Shires, *Rocky Mountain News*

"Alice Hoffman sets in motion another of her modern-day fairy tales, and in so doing she mesmerizes the reader. Clear your calendar before picking up *The Ice Queen*. You will get nothing else done during the day or two it will take you to finish this fluid, lovely novel."   — Lisa Jennifer Selzman, *Houston Chronicle*

"A lush tale of loss and redemption. Hoffman does a masterful job in weaving fairy-tale elements into the fabric of her contemporary characters' lives. . . . Whether evoking the sultry landscape of southern Florida or the layers of ice around the librarian's heart, Hoffman reminds us how little distance there is between magic and mundane."   — Amy Waldman, *People*

"Throughout Alice Hoffman's long career, her prose has shimmered with echoes of myths and fables as her fiction has explored decidedly modern individuals in often gritty situations.... When the mix is right, she's one of contemporary American literature's most satisfying and thoughtful practitioners.... In *The Ice Queen* we come to see that the narrator isn't merely morose and self-absorbed but that she's on a quest to discover the truth about her past.... The little girl beset by malevolent fate grows into a very human godmother who has learned that love can bring comfort as well as catastrophe."
— Wendy Smith, *Los Angeles Times*

"An electrifying novel." — *Cosmopolitan*

"Hoffman writes intelligently and poignantly in the voice of someone who blames herself for an early trauma."
— Dana Kennedy, *New York Times*

"Alice Hoffman has always been able to bewitch a reader.... She strips her vibrant new novel down to the basic elements of a fairy tale.... The narrator's incandescent involvement with Lazarus becomes the core of self-discovery.... This leads to an emotional and literal whirlwind that brings *The Ice Queen* to an ending with the delicate jolt of an enthralling fairy tale."
— Robert Allen Papinchak, *Seattle Times*

"*The Ice Queen* is one of Hoffman's finest novels.... It is proof that the work of talented New England fabulists like Washington Irving continues, unabated, into the twenty-first century."
— Dorman T. Shindler, *Denver Post*

"As always, Hoffman writes beautifully ... achieving a kind of prose poetry that is rare in contemporary fiction."
— Greg Johnson, *Atlanta Journal-Constitution*

"Hoffman's genius allows the lovers to hang in suspended animation until the outside world intrudes, more threatening than the near fatal electrical disruptions that have defined their lives. Less-skilled hands would have left readers awash in sticky metaphors of heat and ice. Have no such fear with the formidable Hoffman. Highly recommended."
— Beth E. Andersen, *Library Journal* (starred review)

"A compelling tale.... A haunting novel." — Jane Black, *More*

"*The Ice Queen* celebrates the marvelous human ability to change from wicked stepsister to fairy godmother.... For true fans, *The Ice Queen* reads as distilled essence of Hoffman's vision." — Anita Sama, *USA Today*

"This new toughness to *The Ice Queen* bodes well for more delicious darkness in Hoffman's books to come."
— Marta Salij, *Detroit Free Press*

"As beautiful as any book Hoffman has written ... with lush language, overflowing sensory images, and an enchanting story.... Hoffman pulls off an ending that is both inevitable and a surprise that leaves readers satisfied."
— Laurie Higgins, *Cape Codder*

"A stellar novel.... Blanketed in prose that has never been dreamier and gloriously vivid imagery, this life-affirming fable is ripe with Hoffman's trademark symbolism and magic, but with a steelier edge.... Both longtime fans and newcomers will relish it." — *Publishers Weekly* (starred review)

"Magic happens when Alice Hoffman writes."
— Chauncey Mabe, *South Florida Sun-Sentinel*

Blackbird House
The Probable Future
Blue Diary
The River King
Local Girls
Here on Earth
Practical Magic
Second Nature
Turtle Moon
Seventh Heaven
At Risk
Illumination Night
Fortune's Daughter
White Horses
Angel Landing
The Drowning Season
Property Of

For Children

The Foretelling
Moondog
(with Wolfe Martin)
Green Angel
Indigo
Aquamarine
Horsefly
Fireflies

THE
ICE
QUEEN

a novel

ALICE
HOFFMAN

BACK BAY BOOKS

LITTLE, BROWN AND COMPANY

New York   Boston   London

Back Bay Books / Little, Brown and Company
Hachette Book Group
1290 Avenue of the Americas, New York, NY 10104
littlebrown.com

Originally published in hardcover by Little, Brown and Company, April 2005
First Back Bay paperback edition, January 2006

Back Bay Books is an imprint of Little, Brown and Company. The Back Bay Books
name and logo are trademarks of Hachette Book Group, Inc.

The publisher is not responsible for websites (or their content)
that are not owned by the publisher.

The characters and events in this book are fictitious.
Any similarity to real persons, living or dead, is coincidental
and not intended by the author.

Ellen Kanner's conversation with Alice Hoffman, which is reprinted in the reading
group guide at the back of this book, first appeared in the *Miami Herald* on April 24, 2005.
Copyright © 2005 Knight Ridder. All rights reserved. Reprinted with permission.

Library of Congress Cataloging-in-Publication Data

Hoffman, Alice.
  The ice queen : a novel / Alice Hoffman. — 1st ed.
      p.   cm.
  ISBN 978-0-316-05859-9 (hc) / 978-0-316-15438-3 (pb) / 978-0-316-30307-1 (special
edition)
  1. Lightning — Fiction.   2. Single women — Fiction.   3. Women librarians —
Fiction. 4. Life change events — Fiction.   5. Near-death experiences — Fiction.   I. Title.

PS3558.O3447I23   2005
813'.54 — dc22   2004026610

10   9   8   7   6   5   4   3   2   1

RRD-C

Book design by Jo Anne Metsch

Printed in the United States of America

THE ICE QUEEN

C H A P T E R

O N E

Snow

I

B E CAREFUL WHAT YOU WISH FOR. I KNOW
that for a fact. Wishes are brutal, unforgiving
things. They burn your tongue the moment
they're spoken and you can never take them
back. They bruise and bake and come back to
haunt you. I've made far too many wishes in my
lifetime, the first when I was eight years old.
Not the sort of wish for ice cream or a party
dress or long blond hair; no. The other sort, the
kind that rattles your bones, then sits in the back

of your throat, a greedy red toad that chokes you until you say it aloud. The kind that could change your life in an instant, before you have time to wish you could take it back.

I was in the wrong place at the wrong time, but don't all stories begin this way? The stranger who comes to town and wreaks havoc. The man who stumbles off a cliff on his wedding day. The woman who goes to look out the window when a bullet, or a piece of glass, or a blue-white icicle pierces her breast. I was the child who stomped her feet and made a single wish and in so doing ended the whole world — my world, at any rate. The only thing that mattered. Of course I was self-centered, but don't most eight-year-old girls think they're the queen of the universe? Don't they command the stars and seas? Don't they control the weather? When I closed my eyes to sleep at night, I imagined the rest of the world stopped as well. What I wanted, I thought I should get. What I wished for, I deserved.

I made my wish in January, the season of ice, when our house was cold and the oil bill went unpaid. It happened on the sixteenth, my mother's birthday. We had no father, my brother and I. Our father had run off, leaving Ned and me our dark eyes and nothing more. We depended on our mother. I especially didn't expect her to have a life of her own. I pouted when anything took her away: the bills that needed paying, the jobs that came and went, the dishes that needed washing, the piles of laundry. Endless, endless. Never ever done. That night my mother was going out with her two best friends to celebrate her birthday. I didn't like it one bit. It sounded like fun. She was off to the Bluebird Diner, a run-down place famous for its roast beef sandwiches and French fries with gravy. It was only a few hours on her own. It was just a tiny celebration.

I didn't care.

Maybe my father had been self-centered; maybe I'd inherited that from him along with the color of my eyes. I wanted my mother to stay home and braid my hair, which I wore long, to my waist. Loose, my hair knotted when I slept, and I worried; my brother had told me that bats lived in our roof. I was afraid they would fly into my room at night and make a nest in my head. I didn't want to stay home with my brother, who paid no attention to me and was interested more in science than in human beings. We argued over everything, including the last cookie in the jar, which we often grabbed at the same time. *Let go! You first!* Whatever we held often broke in our grasp. Ned had no time for a little sister's whims; he had to be bribed into reading to me. *I'll do your chores. I'll give you my lunch money. Just read.*

My mother didn't listen to my complaints. She was preoccupied. She was in a rush. She put on her raincoat and a blue scarf. Her hair was pale. She'd cut it herself, straining to see the back of her head in the mirror. She couldn't afford a real haircut at a salon; still she was pretty. We didn't talk about being poor; we never discussed what we didn't have. We ate macaroni three times a week and wore heavy sweaters to bed; we made do. Did I realize that night was my mother's thirtieth birthday, that she was young and beautiful and happy for once? To me, she was my mother. Nothing less or more. Nothing that didn't include me.

When she went to leave, I ran after her. I was barefoot on the porch and my feet stung. The rain had frozen and was hitting against the corrugated green fiberglass roof. It sounded like a gun. Ice had slipped onto the floorboards and turned the wood to glass. I begged my mother not to go. Queen of the universe. The girl who thought of no one but herself. Now I know the most desperate arguments are always over foolish things. The moment that changes the path of a life is the one that's invisible, that dissolves like sugar in water. But tell that to an eight-year-old girl. Tell it to anyone; see who believes you.

When my mother said that Betsy and Amanda were waiting for her and that she was already late, I made my wish. Right away, I could feel it burning. I could taste the bitterness of it; still I went ahead. I wished I would never see her again. I told her straight to her face. I wished she would disappear right there, right then.

My mother laughed and kissed me good-bye. Her kiss was clear and cold. Her complexion was pale, like snow. She whispered something to me, but I didn't listen. I wanted what I wanted. I didn't think beyond my own needs.

My mother had to start the car several times before the engine caught. There was smoke in the air. The roof of the patio vibrated along with the sputtering engine of the car. I could feel the sourness inside me. And here was the odd thing about making that wish, the one that made her disappear: it hurt.

"Come inside, idiot," my brother called to me. "The only thing you'll accomplish out there is freezing your ass off."

Ned was logical; he was four years older, an expert on constellations, red ants, bats, invertebrates. He had often told me that feelings were a waste of time. I didn't like to listen to Ned, even when he was right, so on that night I didn't answer. He shouted out a promise to read to me, even if it had to be fairy tales, stories he held in contempt. Irrational, impossible, illogical things. Even that wasn't enough for me to end my vigil. I couldn't stop looking at the empty street. Soon enough my brother gave up on me. Didn't everyone? My feet had turned blue and they ached, but I stood out there on the porch for quite a while. Until my tongue stopped burning. When I finally went inside, I looked out the window, and even Ned came to see, but there was nothing out there. Only the snow.

MY MOTHER HAD HER ACCIDENT ON THE SERVICE ROAD leading to the Interstate. The police report blamed icy road conditions and bald tires that should have been replaced. But we were poor, did I tell you that? We couldn't afford new tires. My mother was half an hour late for her birthday dinner, then an hour; then her friend Betsy called the police. The next morning when our grandmother came to tell us the news, I braided my own hair for the first time, then cut it off with a pair of gardening shears. I left it behind for the bats. I didn't care. I'd started to wonder if my brother had been right all along. Don't feel anything. Don't even try.

After the funeral, Ned and I moved into our grandmother's house. We had to leave some of our things behind: my brother his colony of ants, and I left all my toys. I was too old for them now. My grandmother called what I'd done to my hair a pixie cut, but could she give a name to what I'd done to my mother? I knew, but I wasn't saying. My grandmother was too kind a person to know who was living under her roof. I'd destroyed my mother with words, so words became my enemy. I quickly learned to keep my mouth shut.

At night I told myself a story, wordless, inside my head, one I liked far better than those in my books. The girl in my story was treated cruelly, by fate, by her family, even by the weather. Her feet bled from the stony paths; her hair was plucked from her head by blackbirds. She went from house to house, looking for refuge. Not a single neighbor answered his door, and so one day the girl gave up speaking. She lived on the side of a mountain where every day was snowy. She stood outside without a roof, without shelter; before long she was made of ice — her flesh, her bones, her blood. She looked like a diamond; it was possible to spy her from miles away. She was so beautiful now that everyone wanted her: people came to talk to her, but she wouldn't answer. Birds lit on her shoulder; she didn't bother to chase them away. She didn't have to. If they took a single peck, their beaks would break in two. Nothing could hurt her anymore. After a while, she became invisible, queen of the ice. Silence was her language, and her heart had turned a perfect pale silver color. It was so hard nothing could shatter it. Not even stones.

"Physiologically impossible," my brother said the one time I dared to tell him the story. "In such low temperatures, her heart would actually freeze and then burst. She'd wind up melting herself with her own blood."

I didn't discuss such things with him again.

I knew what my role was in the world. I was the quiet girl at school, the best friend, the one who came in second place. I didn't want to draw attention to myself. I didn't want to win anything. There were words I couldn't bring myself to say; words like *ruin* and *love* and *lost* made me sick to my stomach. In the end, I gave them up altogether. But I was a good grandchild, quick to finish tasks, my grandmother's favorite. The more tasks, the less time to think. I swept, I did laundry, I stayed up late finishing my homework. By the time I was in high school, I was everyone's confidante; I knew how to listen. I was there for my friends, a tower of strength, ever helpful, especially when it came to their boyfriends, several of whom slept with me in senior year, grateful for my advice with their love lives, happy to go to bed with a girl who asked for nothing in return.

My brother went to Harvard, then to Cornell for his graduate degree; he became a meteorologist, a perfect choice for someone who wanted to impose logic onto an imperfect world. He was offered a position at Orlon University, in Florida, and before long he was a full professor, married to a mathematician, Nina, whom he idolized for her rational thought and beautiful complexion. As for me, I looked for a career where silence would be an asset. I went to the state university a few towns over, then to City College for a master's in library science. My brother found it especially amusing that my work was considered a science, but I took it quite seriously. I was assigned to the reference desk, still giving advice, as I had in high school, still the one to turn to for information. I was well liked at the library, the reliable employee who collected money for wedding presents and organized baby showers. When a co-worker moved to Hawaii I was persuaded to adopt her cat, Giselle, even though I was allergic.

But there was another, hidden side to me. My realest self. The one who remembered how the ice fell down, piece by bitter piece. The one who dreamed of cold, silver hearts. A devotee of death. I had become something of an expert on the many ways to die, and like any expert I had my favorites: bee stings, poisoned punch, electric shock. There were whole categories I couldn't get enough of: death by misadventure or by design, death pacts, death to avoid the future, death to circumvent the past. I doubted whether anyone else in the library was aware that rigor mortis set in within four hours. If they knew that when heated, arsenic had a garlic-like odor. The police captain in town, Jack Lyons, who'd been in my brother's class in high school, often called for information regarding poison, suicide, infectious diseases. He trusted me, too.

Once I began researching death, I couldn't stop. It was my calling; I suppose it was a passion. I ordered medical texts, entomology books, the Merck manual of pharmaceuticals so as to be well versed in toxic side effects when Jack Lyons called. My favorite reference book was *A Hundred Ways to Die,* a guide for the terminally ill, those who might be in dire need of methods and procedures for their own demise. Still, I always asked Jack if he hadn't someone more qualified than I to do his research, but he said, "I know I'll just get the facts from you. No interpretations."

In that regard, he was wrong. I was quiet, but I had my opinions: when asked to recommend which fairy tales were best for an eight-year-old, for instance, Andersen's or Grimm's, I always chose Grimm's. Bones tied in silken cloth laid to rest under a juniper tree, boys who were foolish and brave enough to play cards with Death, wicked sisters whose own wickedness led them to hang themselves or jump headfirst into wells. On several occasions there had been complaints to the head librarian when irate mothers or teachers had inadvertently scared the daylights out of a child on my recommendation. All the same, I stood my ground. Andersen's world was filled with virtuous, respectable characters. I preferred tales in which selfish girls who lost their way needed to hack through brambles in order to reach home, and thoughtless, heedless brothers were turned into donkeys and swans, fleas itching like mad under their skin, blood shining from beneath their feathers. I didn't believe that people got what they deserved. I didn't believe in a rational, benevolent world that could be ordered to suit us, an existence presumed to fit snugly into an invented logic. I had no faith in pie charts or diagrams of humanity wherein the wicked were divided from the good and the *forever after* was in direct opposition to the *here and now*.

When I walked home from the library on windy nights, with the leaves swirling, and all of New Jersey dark and quiet, I wouldn't have been surprised to find a man with one wing sitting on the front steps of Town Hall, or to come upon a starving wolf on the corner of Fifth Street and Main. I knew the power of a single wish, after all. Invisible and inevitable in its effect, like a butterfly that beats its wings in one corner of the globe and with that single action changes the weather halfway across the world. Chaos theory, my brother had informed me, was based on the mathematical theorem that suggests that the tiniest change affects everything, no matter how distant, including the weather. My brother could call it whatever he wanted to; it was just fate to me.

Before I knew it thirteen years had passed at the library, and then fifteen. I still wore my hair the same way — the haircut I'd given myself at the age of eight had become my trademark. People expected certain things of me: assistance, silence, comfort. They had no idea who I was. I dated Jack Lyons for some of that time, if you could call it that. He'd phone me for information, and later that same evening he'd be waiting for me in the parking lot. We'd do it in his car. The sex was hurried and panicked and crazy, but we did it anyway. We took chances. Times when patrons would be arriving, days when there was so much snow, drifts three feet high built up around the car. Maybe I wanted to get caught, but we never did. We were alone in the world. Jack knew I didn't like to speak; true enough, but it was my own words I mistrusted. No one else's. He could say whatever he liked. He could even blurt out that he loved me, as long as he didn't mean it. That was the important thing. The girl encased in ice facing the mountain. The cold silence that was so clean it didn't hurt. For me, there was nothing beyond those mountains. Nothing worth going toward.

Jack always let me walk home alone and he never tried to follow me. I thought he knew me better than most. I thought he understood I didn't deserve kindness, or loyalty, or luck. Then one night Jack brought me flowers, a handful of fading daisies he'd picked up at a farm stand, but flowers all the same. That was the end; that was how he ruined everything. The minute Jack acted as though we were anything more than two strangers who had a shared interest in death and sex, it was over. As soon as there was the possibility he might actually care for me, I stopped seeing him.

Without Jack, my life was completely uneventful. When the time came, it made sense for me to be the one to tend to my grandmother as she was dying. My brother was busy with his own life in Florida and I had no life at all, only the library, only walking home by myself at night. It was my duty, after all, and my responsibility. My grandmother loved me, truly and deeply, even though the only thing I had given her in return for her affection was chicken soup, toast with butter, pot after pot of English breakfast tea with honey and lemon, and an endless supply of library books. Our house was littered with books — in the kitchen, under the beds, stuck between the couch pillows — far too many for her to ever finish. I suppose I thought if my grandmother kept up her interests, she wouldn't die; she'd have to stay around to finish the books she was so fond of. *I've got to get to the bottom of this one,* she'd say, as if a book were no different from a pond or a lake. I thought she'd go on reading forever, but it didn't work out that way.

"You should be enjoying your life," my grandmother said to me one night while I was helping her with her nightly cup of tea. Even drinking tea was difficult for her. She took little sips, like a bird. I had to hold her head up; she smelled like lemon and dust. I felt like crying, even though that was impossible for me. Crying wasn't like riding a bicycle; give it up and you quickly forget how it's done. Look in the mirror and make faces, cut up onions, watch sorrowful movies. None of that can bring back tears.

That night my grandmother's sudden advice took me completely by surprise. I'd assumed that she of all people understood I'd been ruined long ago. I didn't deserve to be happy. Didn't my dear grandmother understand that? I had already passed the age my mother had been on that icy night when she drove off to meet her friends. Who was I to enjoy anything?

"You're always so negative," my grandmother said.

"You got all the positive genes." Amazing, considering her condition, considering the condition of the world.

Toward the end of her illness, even my grandmother had to face sorrow. She cried in her sleep. I couldn't stand to hear her suffering. I left the cat I'd adopted to keep watch over her, curled up on the hospital bed I'd rented, and I went to stand outside, where I could breathe in the brackish air. It was spring and there was pine pollen everywhere; things had turned a sulfury yellow. That night I wished that my whole life had been different and that I could start all over again, in Paris or London, in Italy, even across the river in New York City, where I'd gone to school. I was still young. I wished I could shed my skin, walk away, never look back. But starting a new life was not my expertise. Death was my talent; before I could stop myself, I wished my grand-mother's pain would end. I wished that this world would no longer have a hold on her.

She died that night while I was sleeping on the couch. The cat was beside her, and when I heard Giselle mewling, I knew what had happened. My brother didn't come up to New Jersey until several days after our grandmother's pass-ing; the funeral had to wait because it was exam week at Orlon University. Ned realized what was happening to me as soon as he walked in the house. I was like a bird that had been let out of its cage only to find it could go no farther than

the windowsill. All those years of planning my escape from
New Jersey, and now I couldn't even leave the living room.
I'd pretty much stopped eating, aside from cornflakes and
milk, which was the only thing I could keep down. I hadn't
showered and I gave off a faint odor of mildew, the scent of
the ruined and the lost. I had called in to the library to let
them know I wouldn't be coming back. The reference desk
was too much for me. Everything was. Jack sent me a sym-
pathy note on police stationery; he wrote that he missed me,
more than he'd ever expected to, and was hopeful I would
soon return to my desk. But that wasn't about to happen.
I could barely find a reason to get dressed, let alone field
meaningless research questions or have sex with someone I
didn't care about in the backseat of his car. Sometimes I sim-
ply stayed in my bathrobe. I had lost the will to wash my
face, to look in the mirror, to step outside, to breathe the air.

My brother and I hadn't had a real conversation in years.
Too busy, lives too far apart. But after the funeral he sat be-
side me on the couch. He was allergic to cats, just as I was,
and his eyes had already begun to water because of Giselle.

"This is not going to do you any good," Ned told me.
"You can't stay here."

Logical still, as if it mattered. Logical then, as well. I
thought of the morning of my mother's death; before my
grandmother had arrived, I'd wandered out in my pajamas
and saw him in the kitchen. I think he might have been
cleaning up. He was orderly even then. *It's too early,* Ned
had told me. *Go back to bed.* I did exactly that. Two days
later we'd sat together, side by side on folding chairs at my
mother's funeral, held at the gravesite. A few of my mother's

friends were there, all in black dresses. Ned wore a black suit, borrowed probably. I'd never seen it before. I had a navy blue dress with a lace collar that I'd snipped off with the same shears I'd used to cut my hair. There was a plain pine coffin, closed. Still, I'd read enough fairy tales to know the dead were not necessarily gone. Our mother might have been asleep, under a spell, ready to rap on the coffin from within and beg, *Let me out!*

It could happen at any time. The sky was gray; there was ice on the ground. And then I saw that Ned was crying. He was quiet about it. He didn't make a sound. I don't think I'd ever seen him do that before, so I quickly looked away. And then the coffin looked different. Shut tight. Over and done.

At my grandmother's service, Ned and I were the only mourners. Same kind of plain pine box, same graveyard. We had never gotten around to putting a marker on my mother's grave, and I was glad of this. I didn't want to know exactly where she'd been buried. Maybe she hadn't been buried at all. Maybe I'd been wrong and she had indeed flung open the wooden box to run through the dark and the cold the moment we'd left the gravesite. I looked for footprints, though it had been more than twenty years. Only the scratch scratch of birds. And something else — the tracks of a fox.

Ned had not only handled my grandmother's affairs, he'd already done the research needed to set my life in order as well. He had found me a job, at the public library in Orlon, and a cottage to rent only a few blocks from the university campus. We debated the merits of a move. Statistically, the odds weren't on Ned's side. Had money been involved, I would have bet my future consisted of twenty more years in my grandmother's house, wearing my bathrobe. But my brother was a worthy opponent, methodical if nothing else, and a challenge never deterred him, even if that challenge was me.

While I was moping about and eating cornflakes, Ned packed up the house, called the real estate agent, had new tires put on my car. And so it was. I was leaving New Jersey. My colleagues wanted to give me a going-away party at the library, but without me, there was no one to organize it. I took the cat with me. I had no choice. Giselle jumped in the car and made herself comfortable on my brother's jacket, ensuring that Ned would sneeze all the way down to Florida.

It was an unseasonably hot day when we left. The air was sulfur-colored, gray around the edges, and the humidity was at 98 percent.

"This will get you used to Florida." Ned was oddly joyful.

There was sheet lightning ahead of us on the New Jersey Turnpike, the silent sort that is so vivid it can light up the whole sky. My brother was delighted by the weather; his department was currently involved in a lightning study and he was one of the project advisers.

"Without thunderstorms, the earth would lose its electrical charge in less than an hour," Ned told me.

He kept notes on the storm as I drove. I was used to being alone, accustomed to talking to myself; without thinking, I made another wish aloud, despite how it burned. I wished lightning would strike me.

"Like hell you do," my brother said. One of the tasks of the meteorology department at Orlon was to work with a team of physicians and biologists, addressing neurological injuries found in lightning-strike victims. "You have no idea of the damage that can be done. None whatsoever."

But it didn't really matter. I had made another death wish, and I could tell what was to come from the bitter taste in my mouth.

It was too late to take it back.

II

THE CAT WASN'T AT ALL HAPPY WITH THE MOVE. I couldn't blame her. Orlon was hardly a paradise. Cats, after all, are creatures of habit, said to become more attached to a place than to a person. This was certainly true of my alleged pet, who had never seemed to miss the original owner from whom I'd inherited her. Not for a moment had she sat by a window, waiting to be rescued. Why, she didn't even seem to recognize the existence of human beings. My prize. My pet.

Giselle, I'd call when she was out in the garden, but she'd only ignore me and flick her tail, as though I were another fly, one of the thousands that seemed to be breeding in Orlon. Even my own cat disliked me. What had I expected? Life was no better here in Orlon, despite what my brother had promised, only hotter, buggier, far more humid than New Jersey at its worst. The library where I found myself employed was underfunded: there was one other librarian, Frances York, who had worked at the same post for forty years and whose eyesight was now failing — hence my job. Untrustworthy as I might be, I was to be her eyes.

This is what I saw: Most of the shelves were empty. Budget cuts. Public's lack of interest. I had more books packed in cartons and left in storage in New Jersey than the Orlon Public Library had in its entirety. There were no computers available to the patrons, only one ancient word processor at the desk, and an old-fashioned card catalog was still in use. As for the reference department, there didn't seem to be one. After several weeks at work, there'd been only three calls of any kind: two concerning the proper use of fertilizer, and a third from a second-grader wanting to know what medical school Dr. Seuss had gone to. Maybe I should have lied to my young caller, but it wasn't in my nature to do so. When I told her that her favorite author wasn't a doctor, that in fact his last name wasn't even Seuss, she hung up on me. I suppose no one had told her before that she mustn't trust words, not even the ones in books.

Because we were a college town, the students at Orlon had their own high-tech facility, so our little building was all but invisible to them. And as our budget didn't allow the purchase of any new editions, even the local folks stayed away. The only weekly activity was the nursery-school reading club, but that group was nearly disbanded after I read "The Goose Girl," a tale in which a truth-teller, a beloved, loyal horse named Falada, continues to speak long after his severed head is mounted on the wall. Frances took back the position of reader, even though she was nearly blind and had to hold a book right up to her face to make out the story.

Frances was polite about my removal, and I understood. Death was my talent, not lively toddlers. I gratefully relinquished the nursery group, happy enough to avoid the rush of noisy little creatures on Thursday afternoons.

During my hours at the library I found myself longing for questions about death. New Jersey had begun to seem like a dream rather than a nightmare. I stared at the phone, missing Jack Lyons and his calls; our longest, most intimate conversations had been about diseases that were spread by mosquitoes, especially West Nile virus. As for my brother, he and Nina were busy with their work at the university; after they'd helped me set up the house — which my brother had failed to mention was not air-conditioned, there was only a ceiling fan — I rarely saw Ned and his wife. I hadn't expected more, and why should I have? They had their own lives, after all.

In the evenings, I listened to the radio and busied myself with killing flies, using a flyswatter I'd bought at Acres' Hardware Store. A bit of death at home. Something I understood. Something I was good at. I'd killed hundreds of flies in no time. I kept piles of bodies on the windowsill. That's what I was doing when it happened. I was holding the flyswatter when I saw something that appeared to be a tennis ball right in front of me. The window was open, the ceiling fan was on, the sky was heavy with heat. I thought perhaps some neighborhood kids had thrown the ball through my window. I didn't care for children of any age or size. I knew how they thought and what they were capable of. I was about to shout out for the culprits to get off my lawn. But then I saw that the ball was oddly bright, so shimmery I had to squint. When my gaze shifted I noticed that the flyswatter I was holding was edged in fire and that the fire was dripping down onto the floor, like a sparkler on the Fourth of July.

I was paralyzed, I think, helpless to do anything but watch as the ball fell to the floor. I heard a huge noise: an explosion of some sort, like a shotgun. I thought of the ice that had ricocheted off the roof when my mother drove away. Death sound. The thud of what cannot be stopped. For a second I thought, *It's the end of the world*. My world, I meant. In a way this was true. In a matter of seconds, everything changed. If I had turned left instead of right, perhaps it wouldn't have happened; if the fly I'd swatted had never come in through a hole in the screen, if I'd never left New Jersey, if a butterfly in South America had never unfurled its wings and with a single beat altered everything, now and forevermore.

When I awoke in the hospital I knew at least part of my wish had come true. I could taste it, the burning flavor of death. The wish I'd made in the car traveling down to Florida had accomplished half of its mission, but I was still half alive. I couldn't move my left side. Arms, legs, trunk, had all been affected. There hadn't been a multi-organ disruption — no kidney or lung effects. But my heart had been affected and there had been neurological damage, the two most frequent causes of mortalities in lightning-strike victims. All the same, I was informed that I was lucky to be in Orlon, where there were more lightning strikes than anywhere else in Florida — glorious Florida, the top state for deaths and injuries caused by lightning. Because of this, the medical care in our county was expert. I was supposed to be grateful for that. I would need physical therapy and a serious relationship with a cardiologist, since my heart now skipped a beat. I could feel it fluttering inside me — torn posterior pericardium, they said. It was as though a bird were trapped inside me, one that belonged in a place outside the cage of my aching ribs.

While I was being told about my condition, with my brother and Nina looking on, the only thing I could concentrate on was the clicking inside my head. That wasn't unusual in cases such as mine, the doctor assured me when he heard my complaint. Neither was my nausea or the pain in my neck or the swelling in my face or the fact that my fingers were numb. But look at all I'd escaped! Pulmonary edema, tympanic membrane rupture — deafness brought on by sound and shock — thermal burns from ignited clothing, serious vascular effects, heart attack, cataracts, lesions on the brain, the eye, the skin.

I had been unconscious for thirty-two hours, hence the IV in my arm. Naturally things were fuzzy. Of course, my brother and Nina looked concerned. And so I didn't mention anything when the nurse came in with a dinner tray. I didn't say a word when I noticed that the Jell-O I was being offered was the color of stones. The nurse herself, not more than twenty-five, appeared to have long white hair. The flowers my brother and his wife had brought me seemed dusted with snow. I understood then. I had completely lost the color red. Whatever had once been red was now cloudy and pale. All I saw was ice; all I felt was the cold of my own ruined self. Perhaps I had an ocular reaction to the heat of the strike — vitreous hemorrhage was one of the many potential effects on the eye, along with corneal scratches and cataracts. Why the absence of a color would affect me so deeply, I had no idea, but I suddenly felt completely bereft. I had lost something before I'd known its worth, and now it was too late.

I stayed in the hospital for nearly two weeks. I didn't see much of my brother, but Nina went daily to my house to feed Giselle. When I was finally allowed out, still using a walker because of the weakness on my left side, Nina picked me up and drove me home. I saw that my sister-in-law had also stocked my refrigerator. I think she may have vacuumed. I understood why my brother had been drawn to her. Nina was logical, a great believer in order, and like my brother, she was not a fan of emotions. She stood there and wrung her hands while I sat on the couch and wept.

"Sorry," I said to Nina. She nodded and waved me on. I kept at it, running through nearly a box of tissues. It was my first cry in a long time, and I overdid it. I sat there sobbing, shudders running through me. Suddenly, I was overwhelmed by everything, a wreck, true enough. My hair had fallen out in clumps and there was that dreadful clicking noise in the back of my head. I still wasn't able to hold down solid food. The doctor had told me the symptoms were similar to someone suffering from radiation poisoning. That's how I felt — to my bones, to my toes — poisoned. All down my afflicted side there was a wrenching sort of feeling, as if something had been twisted. A short in my electrical system, I supposed. My very essence, my inner self was gone. I reached for things and couldn't feel them. It was as though everything solid had slipped away from me. Inside, my heart felt frozen.

The weather was still humid and stifling; no outsider could be prepared for Florida. We weren't even close to summer, still the heat exploded in midair, then settled; it weighed you down. All the same, when Nina asked if I'd like anything, I asked for hot tea. I sat there shivering, colder than ever. Ice in my veins. Ice behind my eyes as well, it seemed. While my sister-in-law fixed the tea, I looked out the window. Everything out there was the color of ice. I wondered if the bougainvillea was scarlet: I'd never noticed it before. Now the vine was pale and ghostly, frostbitten and shivering in the heat. I felt as though I had one foot in this world, and one in the next. I couldn't even get the death wish right this time around. I was like a person who'd tried to commit suicide by jumping out a third-story window, succeeding only in breaking every bone. Still alive, still more or less intact, still trapped in the same life.

Before she left, Nina told me a physical therapist would be coming to see me. When the therapist appeared the next morning and rang the bell, I didn't open the door. Maybe I didn't want to be healed. Maybe I deserved whatever I got. Maybe this was the fate I deserved. I sat on the couch with Giselle, imagining I was safe from the well-meaning and the helpful. But my brother had an extra key, which he'd handed over, and the physical therapist let herself in. She introduced herself as Peggy Travis. As though I cared. As though I intended to make this personal. I suppose Peggy was wearing a red striped dress, but it was gray to me. She went through the list of exercises we'd be doing to strengthen my left side. I excused myself. Fumbling with my walker, I went to the bathroom and threw up.

"It's very common to feel sick." My unwelcome visitor had actually come up behind me and was watching me vomit. "For some people it lasts only a short time, for others it's different."

She shut up then. But I got the drift. For others it's an eternity.

I was pathetic really. I couldn't even squeeze a rubber ball. More clumps of my hair fell out just from the stress of trying. But my Peggy wasn't the type to let her charges give up. She had seen it all in working with her clients — the lame, the frail, the screwed-up, the messed-up, the chewed-up, the burnt, the sorrowful. She told me about them when we had tea — hers iced, mine steaming. I'd sweated and grunted through my workout, with my swollen face swelling even more and the clicking going on nonstop; I hardly felt up for conversation. That's how people like Peggy got to you; they waited till you had no defenses, then talked you to death. I felt like a time bomb, as a matter of fact, but I drank my tea. I had no choice but to listen. I heard about Peggy's last client, a man who'd been mauled by a bulldog. By the time the attack was over, the victim had only three fingers, total, and I should have seen how quickly he'd improved. He was now working at Acres' Hardware Store. Before that, it was a woman in a car crash who couldn't remember her own name and needed to be spoon-fed but was now up and about and taking art history classes at Orlon University.

I knew exactly what Peggy was up to. *So take that! See there! You can do it, too! Up by your bootstraps! Work a little harder!*

All of Peggy's cases were success stories. Perhaps I should

have warned her: her luck was about to change. I was stubborn; I suppose I tried to fail, and yet I did improve slightly, at least on the surface. I never mentioned the lack of the color red, the buzzing under my skin, the clicking in my head. The one creature I couldn't hide my most secret effects from was the cat. Sometimes Giselle would come to sit next to me and place her paw on my arm. Her paw would vibrate violently and after an instant, she'd remove it and stare at me. I thought she knew me then. The only creature in the universe that understood how I really felt. No wonder she disliked me. I hadn't fooled her one bit.

Frances York had promised to keep my job open for me at the library, that bookless, underused place. When she telephoned to tell me the news I said, *Oh joy.* She missed the sarcasm; she thought I meant it.

But of course I will, dear. We stick together.

I didn't know if she meant librarians, or losers, or women who were alone, facing some sort of tragedy. I figured she'd had tragedies of her own, not that I wanted to hear about them. I wanted to tell her that at my last job I used to have meaningless sex with someone in the library parking lot on a regular basis. Someone I didn't love and didn't want to love me. That I did it even in the winter, when there was ice everywhere and our breath steamed up the car windows. I wanted to tell her that ever since my lightning strike I spent my nights vomiting and clicking, and that my eyes — the stand-ins for her failing vision — hurt so badly I'd probably never read another book again. I wanted to tell her I had managed to do away with nearly all of the people I loved most in the world, death by proximity and idle wishes, and I still couldn't manage to get rid of myself. Instead, I said, *Thank you,* and promised I'd advise her about my condition; as soon as I felt up to it, I'd come back to the library.

My life was empty and that was fine. It was what I was used to. Yet there was something expected of me, like it or not. I was to be a part of the lightning-strike study, persuaded by my brother to be among the dozens of patients tested by a team of biologists, neurologists, and meteorologists on the third floor of the Science Center over at the university. My brother seemed to feel guilty about what had happened to me, and yet he was avoiding me. Best not to see what disturbs you. Best to order it, examine it, and place it in a study. The way I saw it, chaos theory was at the root of Ned's guilt. On those occasions when he phoned me, it was to discuss the probabilities of my lightning strike. If he hadn't insisted, I wouldn't have moved to Florida. If I hadn't moved, I wouldn't have been struck, and on and on. I didn't want to hear any more and I certainly didn't want to see Ned suffer. One of us doing that was enough.

So I gave in.

The experts tapped at me, charted my heartbeat, examined my skeleton. I saw a neurologist. A cardiologist. Then a psychologist. They gave me a battery of intelligence tests and told me it was fine if I didn't remember the names of historical figures most fifth-graders could reel off. There were psychological tests as well; I expected as much. On those questions I answered that everything was false.

I was informed that there were many different kinds of lightning strikes — splash, contact, step voltage, blunt trauma, and direct hit. Mine seemed to have been a splash —

the flyswatter, it seemed, had come between me and the full force of what can be as much as 120 million volts. Ninety percent of lightning-strike victims survived, but 25 percent suffered major effects, some of which weren't apparent for months or even years. My brother sent over several books, and the medical staff loaded me down with pamphlets. I think they were all trying not just to educate me but to let me know how lucky I was simply to be alive.

By the end of the month, the neurologist in charge of my case, Dr. Wyman, said I was progressing nicely. I knew I wasn't. Oh, I had moved on from a walker to a cane, from physical therapy every day to twice a week and finally to practicing my exercises alone. Peggy had gone on to her next patient, an elderly man who'd fallen down the stairs and broken every single bone in his legs. I was done as far as Peggy was concerned. *Up and about and enjoying the Florida weather,* I'm sure she was saying to the man with broken bones. Dr. Wyman was most likely discussing me with his colleagues. *Such good progress!* Even when I admitted the ocular problem, he insisted the fading of a single color was nothing to worry about. Perhaps to him it was nothing, but to me the loss of red was staggering; the emptiness I was left with made me weep. In my world, a cherry was no different from a stone. Oh, how I missed things that had never mattered to me before. An apple, a carnation, a bird I knew to be a cardinal, which to my eyes was as gray as a dove.

There were no words for how wrong Wyman was in his assessment of my condition. In fact, I'd been deteriorating. The crying, the coldness inside, the fear every time I walked out the door. How could I tell the doctor what was wrong with me? I didn't understand it myself. I couldn't articulate the pain; it was the pain of nothingness. My fear was of the weather, the atmosphere, the very air. What good did safety tips do me now? *Avoid water, metal objects, rooftops; stay off the telephone in a storm; don't think glass can protect you; even if a storm is eight miles away, you're still not safe from a strike.* Avoid life, perhaps that was the answer. The number one safety tip. *Stay away from it all.*

Without words, only action would do. To show my doctor what little progress I'd made, to show him what my world was made of, I put my hand through the window. It was a staggeringly stupid thing to do, but maybe Peggy had been right. Maybe I wanted help; maybe I was desperate for it. I was trapped behind glass, cold, empty, dead inside. Such was my condition, Doctor, if you really want to know: shattered.

The Science Center was cool, crisp, temperature-controlled. It was a shock to have broiling hot air stream through the broken window into the deeply cold room. The doctor leapt back. Glass covered the floor, shimmering. In all honesty, I had stunned myself. It was as though the girl in my childhood story had suddenly lurched forward against her casing of blue ice.

"Good Lord!" Wyman said. "What do you think you're doing?"

Blood, I suppose, was running down my arm. It looked like paste to me.

"Are you crazy?" my doctor asked me.

That didn't seem a very professional question. And frankly, I thought it was up to Wyman to tell me. He was the diagnostician, after all; he was the one so certain I was improving.

The maintenance crews were mowing the grass, and the humming of their work mixed with the click inside my head, so I stopped listening to the doctor. I was taken back to the hospital in an ambulance, even though all I needed was a few stitches. I had just wanted to get my point across. What was so wrong about that? There it was, every bit of who I was: blood, panic, sorrow. Did I have to spell it out for him?

I was observed by internists and a psych team for forty-eight hours, during which time I made certain to be extremely pleasant. I could do that whenever I wanted to. I'd learned how in high school. The *me* you want me to be, the girl who knows how to listen. It didn't take long before the nurses were confiding in me about their love lives, just as my friends had in high school. The dietitian took a special liking to me. Her mother was dying; she closed the door so she could cry in front of me. I didn't tell her about my own history, my mother running to her car, my dear grandmother crying in her sleep.

But all the time I was in the psych ward, I might as well have been made of ice. That first crying jag I'd had was surely an anomaly. In the ward, I looked in the distance for mountains, but there were only meshed windows, tall cabbage palms. The things I was most aware of were the things I was unable to see: geraniums in pots along the windowsill, gray and black checkers set out on drab boards, the mouths of the nurses as they spoke to me, lips so icy white they seemed frozen.

When they released me — progress, again! — I took a cab home. I found Giselle pacing at the door, ravenous. This time Nina had forgotten her, so I fed the poor creature tuna fish from the can and a saucerful of milk. My diagnosis was panic disorder and depression, and I couldn't agree more. Trauma-induced, they told me. Well, yes, that was true. Only the trauma hadn't happened here in Florida, and it had nothing to do with lightning.

When I let the cat out in the yard I could feel the change in the atmosphere. It was the oddest thing. It was as though I were a cloud instead of a human being. I knew it would start raining minutes before it did. I could feel the charged atoms in the air, and I was quick to call Giselle in before her coat got matted and wet. While I was getting into bed there was a lightning strike nearly five miles away. The strike split a pine tree in two and started a fire that burned several houses down to ash. It was summer lightning, the kind that appears without thunder, without a sign. But I didn't need anyone to tell me about it.

It was the one thing I could feel deep inside.

Light

I

W HAT'S THE DIFFERENCE BETWEEN LIGHT-

ning and magic? is a joke common among me-

teorologists.

Magic makes sense. Lightning does not, even

to the experts. Lightning is random, unpredict-

able. It can be as small as a bean or as large as

a house. Noisy or silent, ashy or clear. It can be

any color — red or white, blue or smoky black —

and it seems to have a mind of its own. Light-

ning floats down chimneys and enters closed

windows, slipping right through the molecules that make up glass. Lightning has its own agenda, most experts say; it can easily cause damage despite all safety efforts. Hide, but it may find you. Plan, but your plan may easily become undone.

Lightning plays favorites, picking the one out of the many, singling certain people out of groups of hundreds, even thousands. Lightning plays pranks, and seems to enjoy them. Lightning reaches 50,000 degrees Fahrenheit, more than five times the heat of the sun. It can be a hundred miles long, as thin as a man's pinkie. Its effects are puzzling and indiscriminate. There are trees that have been hit that show no effect and then, months later, suddenly wither. Doors are removed from their hinges; cars are set on fire, and afterward only the radio is found to be working, crooning a sad song. People safe in their houses, chatting on the phone, have had lightning come in through the wires, entering the earpiece to strike them deaf. In one case a dog that had been struck farted black sulfur for weeks. Hairpieces have been snatched off bald men's heads, women have been stripped of their clothes, children have reported seeing flaming objects circling their rooms, only to be disbelieved until all the electricity goes out or the walls themselves catch fire.

Some people get up after a strike and finish their golf games, go about their business, have quite a story to tell. Others' lives are forever ruined.

Is that magic? Does it make any sense? Most incidents of odd weather can be logically explained. Blood rains, once thought to be the wrath of the heavens, are actually made up of the mecondial fluids released by certain lepidoptera simultaneously emerging from their chrysalides. Black rains, those old wives' tales, are in fact stones picked up in whirlwinds and released elsewhere. Frogs falling from the sky, same thing, no magic whatsoever; the poor creatures are simply swept up in one place by a windstorm, then deposited on the shores of another land. And what if these frogs open their mouths and pearls fall out? Even then logic prevails: the frogs have probably been air-lifted from the China Seas, home of pearls shining in a dozen different shades no one would never expect: red, scarlet, crimson. Pearls the color of a human heart.

At Orlon University, the team was working backward, trying to understand lightning by studying its effects on human physiology. Our group of survivors met in the cafeteria of the Science Center in the evenings. Summer school wasn't yet in session; for now the campus was quiet. I didn't believe in support groups; why should I go? Nothing could save me. All the same, my brother insisted the group was part of the study I had committed to. It was for the greater good, something I rarely considered. Ned called repeatedly to suggest that for once I finish something I'd started. He had a point, I suppose. But I had no desire to walk across the Orlon campus, however deserted it might be, with my hair falling out, still in need of a cane to steady my limp. I pronounced it *imp,* and it felt that way. An *imp* in my nervous system, pinching at this and that. Reminding me of who I was and who I'd never be.

I might have backed out at the last minute, unintentionally forgotten the time, the day, the location of the meeting, but Ned sent me a report he knew would intrigue me. It was a folder titled *The Naked Man.* How could I resist?

The Naked Man had been a roofer — a dangerous occupation, I knew from reading my safety tips. He was working after hours on his mother-in-law's house on the occasion of his strike. He was forty-four years old, six foot two, 240 pounds. He was balding and wore a beard. He'd had two beers at the time of the incident, but he certainly wasn't drunk. He worked alone. He'd never won the lottery, never owned a dog, never made a promise he hadn't kept. Until recently.

That evening he was singing Johnny's Cash's "Ring of Fire." Later, he realized this particular song was on his mind because he was having an affair with a woman who worked at the Smithfield Mall. Johnny Cash's wife had written "Ring of Fire" when they fell in love and were married to other people. There was desire in that song, big-time. That was probably why the roofer was fixing his mother-in-law's roof on such a dismal night. Guilt and desire, a bad combination. Storms were predicted, but he figured he had time. He figured a good deed might make up for his failings.

He was mistaken.

Halfway through his work, he heard a hissing sound, and he found himself thinking of hell and whether or not he might end up there, if such a place existed. His fingers started to tingle. And then he saw what he thought was the moon falling from the sky. But the moon had a tail, and that was surely a bad sign. It was ball lightning; it fell on the roof and rolled down toward him. It looked like a comet headed straight for him, a blue-black thing that was as solid and real as a truck or a boot or a living, breathing man. The roofer thought he might be face-to-face with the devil himself, that fallen angel. He thought about everything he hadn't yet done in his life. All of a sudden owning a dog seemed like the most important thing in the world.

The hissing got louder and the next thing the roofer knew, he was standing on the grass, completely naked except for his work boots. His clothes were a pile of ashes and his beard was gone. In the photographs in his file, the Naked Man is standing against a white screen; he looks like a baby, wide-eyed, just welcomed to the world. My brother knew I'd have to see him in person. I was a librarian, after all; I'd want to know how the story ended. Had he gotten his dog? Had he ended his affair? Had he found another line of work, one that wasn't so close to the sky?

I spied the Naked Man as soon as I entered the cafeteria. He seemed to have lost weight since he'd been struck. He used a cane, as I did. Surely the *imp* was in his system, definite neurological damage, but he was the silent type. He stared straight ahead, and I had the notion that he'd been coerced into coming, the way I'd been. Someone had insisted it would be good for him, cathartic, as if anything could be.

Most people in the group were more than happy to talk about their effects — that's what they called their symptoms. The Naked Man kept silent, but the others were studying themselves, as if each one was a singular chemical experiment gone awry. After what they'd been through, who could blame them really? They didn't whine or complain; they were matter-of-fact. Most, like me, had headaches and

nausea and disorientation. Some had effects that kept them
from working, from sleeping, from thinking straight, from
having sex. There were myths that lightning-strike victims
became hypersexual, electrified, in a manner of speaking,
but most often there was the opposite effect — impotence
and depression. Some in the group shook with muscle
spasms, and some stuttered; some looked perfectly normal,
and maybe they were. There were plenty of memory glitches,
lost thoughts, forgotten identities. One fellow couldn't re-
member where he'd been born. A girl couldn't recall her
middle name. For most, the moments before their strikes
were the clearest time of their lives. Just as they would have
remembered the stars falling from the sky, the memory of
that bright instant was something they couldn't get rid of, no
matter how hard they might try.

I noticed the man next to me, a boy really, in his early
twenties. Tall, gawky, hazel eyes. Oddly enough, wearing
gloves. When he caught me looking, he leaned over, close.

"Want to see?"

The clicking in my head was bad; I may have nodded. I
suppose he took that as a yes and thought I wanted to find
out what was under those gloves. As if I cared. The boy's
name was Renny, and he was a sophomore at Orlon about to
attend summer classes, trying to make up for the semester
he'd lost when he was hit. When he took off his gloves I
could see that he had been wearing a ring on one hand when
he'd been struck by lightning, a watch on the other. Both
pieces of jewelry had left deep indentations in his skin, as
though he'd been branded by the heated metal. He didn't
have to say his hands caused him great pain; that much was

evident from the depth of the ridges, from the way he moved, so tentatively.

"Too bad the watch doesn't tell time," Renny joked. On with his gloves. He winced. "I was on a golf course. Did you know that five percent of strikes take place on golf courses?"

"Really?" These people couldn't talk enough about their experiences.

"I was with all the guys in my fraternity, nearly fifty of us; it was a party, kind of a fund-raiser to fix up our house. We were having a great time and then *kerblam*. I was the only one who got hit. Went right through my head and out my foot. Direct hit. I still have a hole here somewhere." He fingered the top of his head till he found it. "Got it."

The entire interchange was getting much too personal. Next he'd want to know if I slept without a nightgown. If my lightning strike was in my dreams. If I panicked and locked the door at the first sign of rain.

Still, he was grinning at me. I supposed I had to give him something.

"I was in my living room. The flyswatter I was holding caught fire."

That seemed to please him. Almost as though I was confiding in him.

"Wow. I'll bet that was a surprise."

He was so concerned and friendly, I decided to give him a bit more information.

"It was a plastic flyswatter, so it actually started to melt. I bought it at Acres' Hardware Store. It was a splash event." I hoped that sounded professional.

"Good thing you weren't using a rolled-up newspaper. You probably would have ignited."

I liked his habit of understatement. Now when he smiled, I might have smiled back at him.

There were eight of us there that night — old and young, male and female, with nothing to define us, nothing in common. Watching over us, guiding us, I suppose, were a nurse, a neurologist — clearly junior to Dr. Wyman — and a therapist. I was soon to learn that out of all the documented cases of lightning strikes in the state, two-thirds had occurred in Orlon County. Lucky us. We were in the center of all the bad weather in Florida. No wonder my brother was delighted to live here.

We were forced to go around in a circle, introducing ourselves — first names only, of course — with the opportunity to discuss how we were *feeling.* Now everyone clammed up. Physical ailments were one thing, but this was something else entirely. *What has your strike done to your soul? Your sex life? Now that flames have shot through you, is your ego intact? Or is it busy clicking, shaking, shuddering?*

No one spoke up. The Naked Man made himself busy adjusting his boots. A teenaged girl with beautiful curly hair and mismatched socks closed her eyes and hummed. Her face was scarred with what I later learned had been raindrops vaporizing on her skin during her strike, turning to steam and burning her perfect complexion.

We weren't about to talk about our emotional state. No one wanted to get that personal. We eyed one another and laughed self-consciously.

"Next topic," a chicken farmer named Marv called out; he was roundly applauded.

We moved on to what folks really wanted to talk about. Lightning gossip was extremely popular with this group. "Bigger than," "worse than," "did you ever hear of" kind of stories. I listened to the tale of a man who'd been killed by a strike, then carried forty feet and deposited in a haystack. Another of a woman who had every other plate in her china cabinet shatter when lightning came sweeping through her condominium. I learned that open fields were dangerous, that some lightning left rooms filled with smoke, that cows were often victims of a strike, and those who survived gave curdled, yellow milk. But the subject people were most interested in and the stories most often told were about folks who'd been killed and came back to life.

There was a theory, unproven, but accepted by many in the room: the theory of suspended animation. Because lightning was capable of shutting off the systemic and cerebral metabolisms of a victim, much like a short circuit, a person could be "gone" — be officially and medically dead — for an extreme amount of time, past what might seem logically salvageable, and then brought back. Why it was possible to resuscitate such people was unknown. All the same, it happened.

There was an old man near Jacksonville, for example, known as the Dragon, who had allegedly been killed twice by lightning, not that anyone had ever seen him in person. And even closer, a man they called Lazarus Jones, right here in Orlon County. He was definitely real, his existence documented at the morgue and the hospital. Seth Jones, that had been his name before he revived.

I felt something go through my body. A current. It was the mention of an individual who could face down death. All at once, I was interested in something.

That hadn't happened to me for a very long time.

So, what could he do, this man who'd been dead? How big? How bad? I leaned in, the better to hear, dragged my chair closer to the inner circle. Well, for one thing, it was said Lazarus could make an egg on a tabletop spin in a circle. His presence caused electromagnetic disruptions; elevators went up instead of down, lightbulbs burned out, clocks stopped. He'd been five foot ten when struck, six foot afterward. The lightning had stretched him, rearranged whoever he'd been before, altering him almost beyond recognition. He now radiated so much heat, he could eat only cold food; anything raw became cooked as he swallowed. He'd been gone for forty minutes, no heartbeat, no pulse. Impossible, of course, and yet it was true, documented by the EMTs. When Lazarus arose, his eyes were so black it was impossible to tell whether his pupils were dilated. Not that he would let anyone test him. Not eyes nor heart nor lungs.

"How did he manage to come back to life?" I asked Renny. "Wouldn't he be brain-damaged after all that time?"

"Not if the theory of suspended animation holds true."

We were whispering, knee against knee. I could feel Renny had a tremor. If I wasn't careful, I'd start feeling sorry for him.

"They've been trying to study this guy Jones, but he won't talk to the folks at Orlon. I guess he's super-paranoid. I heard he chased Dr. Wyman off his property with a gun."

Wyman, the neurologist who'd wanted to know if I was crazy when I put my hand through the window.

"Maybe he's got the right idea," I ventured. "Wyman's my doctor, too. Maybe we shouldn't be such guinea pigs."

"Oh, I don't mind. At least they give us snacks. And not just carrots."

Renny grinned, then got up and headed to the refreshment table. I saw that he, too, limped. The foot the lightning had gone through had shriveled and was misshapen and the leg seemed to have nerve damage. Hence the tremor, the wobbling when he walked. I looked away. I didn't want to think about Renny lining up his putt on the green, out for a great day, nothing more.

I wanted things cold, the way they'd always been. And yet, I felt moved by these people in some way I didn't understand. Perhaps it was because each one was ruined so uniquely, every undoing so against all probability. I turned and saw that the Naked Man was sitting with his head in his hands, eyes closed. He was sleeping. A woman next to me, struck while pruning her hedges, held a finger to her lips.

"Poor thing," she whispered.

I noticed that the Naked Man wasn't wearing a wedding band, that there was dog hair on his pant leg, short black hair, probably a Labrador retriever. Maybe he'd gotten what he'd wanted, or what he'd imagined he'd wanted. But he moaned in his sleep, and we all turned to him, startled by the sound. There it was, like a toad let out in a garden. Sorrow.

The Naked Man didn't open his eyes until the group was breaking up. Then he told us this sleep disorder was happening to him more and more; he couldn't stay awake. He would be having a conversation with someone, and the next thing he knew, he'd be fast asleep, snoring. He couldn't tell the difference between his life and a dream. That was his problem. He'd talk to his girlfriend, Marie, about what they'd done the day before, and she'd look blank. Then he'd understand — it hadn't been real. The canoe on the river, the car on the road, the storm or the clear sky he'd been so certain of, all of it disappeared as soon as he opened his eyes.

"I want to be awake," the Naked Man said. "That's all I'm asking for."

We all looked away when he started to cry. I, for one, hoped he would remember this as a dream. A hazy room of stunned and silent people who were decent enough to give him his privacy. Before he knew it, he'd be out walking his dog and he wouldn't even remember us, the strangers who wished the best for him, who wished he would indeed wake up.

We all had our photographs taken that night. It was part of the study. Quite necessary, we were told. One by one, we went into the examining room. We took off our clothes and stood in front of a white screen. As I stood there shivering, I recalled a fairy tale, "The Boy Who Went Forth to Learn What Fear Was." It was a tale I'd disliked as a child about a boy who is so brave he can play cards with corpses and subdue ghouls without ever once flinching. When my brother read to me, I always insisted he skip right over to the next one. I didn't like stories in which Death was a major character. Even for me, this tale seemed too illogical. Who on earth could look at death and be unafraid?

When my time came to be photographed I got into

position and did as I was told. I turned left and then right. I kept my spine against the white paper. My photographs would go in my file, the same as everyone else's. My expression would resemble the Naked Man's — blinking in the cold brightness. Maybe that was what kept Lazarus Jones away. He who had no fear, who had wrestled with death and returned far stronger than he'd been before. He wanted his privacy; some people believed a man who told his secrets was a man who lost his strength, and maybe Lazarus Jones was such a man.

I got dressed slowly. I was the last to go. I had just started driving again, which was probably foolish. I wasn't yet well. Sometimes I felt so nauseated I had to pull over to the side of the road to vomit. Once, I had found myself on the highway out of town and I wondered how I'd gotten there, and how I'd ever find my way back.

Coming home from the survivors' meeting, I circled round my block twice before I recognized my own front yard. There it was: the worst lawn on the block, weedy and in need of watering. I pulled into the driveway, hurried inside, went into my bedroom. I took off my clothes and looked in the mirror. I'd closed my eyes when I'd been photographed, as though that could keep who I was and what I looked like from my own consciousness. Now I saw. There was a splotch above my heart, the spot where the lightning had made contact before it sputtered and fell to the floor. I touched that place; inside it was hard, as if a little stone had been implanted beneath the skin.

The windows were open and I could feel the weather outside filtering through the screens. For once, I had good luck.

Unlike the mythical Dragon people spoke of, Lazarus Jones was said to be only fifty miles outside of Orlon. I thought about how the Boy with No Fear had played cards with the dead, how he'd grinned and thrown an ace on the table, how he'd walked through graveyards without a single shiver, how he knew death from the inside out. I wanted a man like that, one it was impossible to kill, who wouldn't flinch if you wished him dead, who'd already been there and back.

I HAD BROUGHT A SUITCASE OF CLOTHES WITH ME TO FLOR-ida, woolen clothes, New Jersey clothes, mittens, scarves, and sweaters. I needed something new for this occasion. I hadn't been shopping for years, not since my grandmother had first taken ill. My clothes were serviceable, suitable for someone ten years older than I. I didn't even have a decent pair of shoes, only flip-flops and sneakers and a pair of snow boots I'd surely never need again. But looking for something to wear in Orlon wasn't so easy. I had to drive to the Smith-field Mall, three exits away on the Interstate.

I'd left my cane at home, and just getting across the park-ing lot in ninety-eight-degree heat took most of my energy. Still I went on, avoiding the Kmart — which I quickly judged as too large and unmanageable. I found a small dress shop and went in. I let the salesgirls bring me outfits while I stayed in the dressing room. It was dark and cold and I think everyone in the shop pitied me. I let them think I was a cancer survivor; it was easier to accept than the truth: the living room, the fireball, the burning flyswatter, the way fate had singled me out.

One of the salesgirls happened to bring in an armful of potential outfits while I was undressed. She took one look at me and sat down on the stool in the corner.

"Sorry." I was apologizing for my own body. I grabbed the first dress on the pile and pulled it on.

"Lightning strike," the salesgirl said. She'd noticed the mark above my heart. "I know it when I see it. Good Lord, I'm living with it every day."

"You?" I asked.

"Him," she told me. "My boyfriend. And he's just about driving me crazy with all of his goddamn effects."

The salesgirl's nametag said Marie. And then I knew who she was. The Naked Man's true love. The one he'd been thinking about up on the roof. I knew too much about her beloved. It might have been embarrassing if I wasn't so used to being in that position.

"The world is a cruel place," Marie told me. "You think you're getting what you want, and you wind up with a plate full of crap." She nodded to my reflection. "That one looks real good," she said of the dress I had on. "I'll give you a ten percent discount for all you've been through."

I turned to the mirror. It was simple, a white shift. Not bad. I thought about the Naked Man's desires, what he'd wanted most at the moment when it seemed death was coming for him.

"Do you have a dog?" I asked Marie.

"A dog? Do you think I'm going to have something shed all over my house? Not likely." She got back to the business at hand. She was like that, concentrated on what was right in front of her. I was starting to think the Naked Man had a secret life, one Marie knew nothing about. "I don't think you're going to look much better than this," Marie told me as she considered my image in the mirror.

I figured she was right. I bought the dress, along with a pair of sandals, and wore them out of the store. I tore off the tags in the car and then I sat there recuperating from my efforts, air-conditioning turned on full blast. I had that tingling feeling in my fingers that the neurologists said was perfectly normal, given that I'd been hit by so much voltage.

I pulled myself together and got back on the Interstate. The only thing I knew for certain was that my tires were safe. Even if my brother seemed to be avoiding me lately, at least he'd spent a great deal of time looking through a consumer's handbook before buying my new tires in New Jersey. I wasn't about to skid, so I drove fast.

Everything looked the same on the road. There were white egrets picking at trash. The grass had turned brown in the heat. We were moving into summer, the season people in Orlon referred to as hell on earth. They laughed about it, though, and none of them seemed intent on moving anyplace cooler. I kept the air-conditioning on in the car, but I opened all the windows. Fresh air in these parts was like a blast from a furnace. My dress blew up and I couldn't hear the clicking in my head so badly with all that wind.

One of my "effects" was that I had to pee all the time. Again, perfectly normal, I was assured. I stopped at a gas station where there were a couple of guys hanging out, drinking sodas, passing the time. They whistled at me. They did, and I really had to laugh. I waved at them. I figured I must have entered the land where there were no women if a pathetic specimen like me drew whistles. I didn't look at myself in the restroom mirror. I just peed and got out of there.

I had looked up Seth Jones's address in the phone book, then gotten myself a local map of Orlon County. All the same, my destination was farther out in the country than I'd thought. Florida was bigger than New Jersey, and people drove more. It didn't seem to bother them one bit, just like the heat, like lightning, like the anole lizards you'd find skittering around your trash cans. When people told you a place was close by, it could be a hundred miles away. I just made up my mind to forget about the time. What had time ever done for me? When I finally got off the Interstate there were groves of fruit trees on either side of the road. The road got smaller, the groves got bigger. Lemons, oranges, and then the signpost for Jones's property. This was where it had happened. In a few days it would be the one-year anniversary of his strike. I had found the article in an old issue of the *Orlon Journal* stacked down in the basement of the library, just a brief report in the Metro section. Several people on the Interstate who saw the flash said it appeared to be going straight, east to west, as though a rocket had been fired. A huge rainstorm followed, leaving an inch of rain in less than an hour. Someone driving past the Jones property saw a deep hole in the ground and steaming black smoke rising.

An ambulance was dispatched and the EMTs who first arrived declared the victim dead at 4:16 P.M. There was no heartbeat, no pulse, no breath. They tried to get his heart started, but no luck. The dead man was delivered to the morgue in the basement, and forty minutes after the lightning struck, the technician on duty turned to see the victim's chest rise and fall beneath the plastic sheet. He was rushed to intensive care. His fingers and toes were black with soot and he was sizzling, hot to the touch. His heartbeat was still sluggish, so they put him in a tub of ice, hoping to shock his system into starting up. It worked. The victim groaned, shivered, and lifted himself out of the tub, demanding his clothes and his boots. Mr. Jones left the hospital an hour later, having refused all services, walking away toward a bus stop.

Another man would have been brain-damaged, if he managed to come back at all. But Lazarus Jones got on the bus and went home. Some people figured it was the ice that had kept his organs intact; others said his return was a miracle. Or maybe it was a sham. Maybe he'd never even been dead at all but was like some of those magicians or yogis you heard about; maybe he had the ability to lower his heart rate and stop his breathing as he hovered in between worlds without a gulp or a gasp.

Forty minutes, that was how long he was gone. From here to there and back again. It had taken me longer to drive from Orlon out here to the country.

The first thing I noticed after I'd turned into the long dirt driveway was the hole in the ground. Not only was it still there, it was much larger than the newspaper had reported — maybe three feet wide. Several trees had been uprooted by the crumbling earth and had recently fallen. Those that were still standing next to the strike spot were odd; the fruit appeared white, like snowballs. I suppose to anyone without my loss of vision, they were a brilliant orangey red. I stopped the car, got out, and took a piece of fruit that had fallen onto the ground. I half expected it to be cold, but it was warm, fragrant. I tore it open and tasted it. I felt like a person without sight who suddenly touched the face of someone she'd been to bed with but had never actually seen. The total surprise of knowing something utterly and completely, the familiar taste of an orange. I ate every bit.

I wiped my hands on my new dress and got back into the car. I drove a little farther, then stopped when I could see the house. It was nothing special. An old farmhouse with a tin roof. The rain, when it came, surely sounded like shotgun pellets; hail, when it fell, surely hammered away. I sat in my car for forty minutes, the exact amount of time he'd been dead. I wanted to get a feel for how long it had been, if that was possible. Could forty minutes be an eternity? Could you walk into fear as one person and come back as someone else entirely? I thought about the morning when I woke up and my mother was gone. The ice on the window glass. The slant of the sunlight. My brother cleaning the kitchen, his back to me. *Go back to bed,* he'd said. *It's too early.* And so I had. I'd dreamed of snow and ice until I heard my grandmother calling my name.

Now I was in a place where there were white oranges in a field. Where there were thin wisps of high clouds. I still felt the wish I had made so long ago. It had been there all along, settled in my chest, in the place where my heart should have been, just below my strike mark.

All I wanted was to be somebody else. Was that asking too much? Was that asking for everything? That's why I was here. It was already happening, just by driving fifty miles. The person I'd been would have never approached a stranger's front door and knocked, not once but three times. Once for ice. Twice for snow. Three for the tires on the road.

Everything smelled hot; dust rose up and burned my nose each time I breathed in. I was someplace where there had never been ice. Where a January day was the same as July. Like the roofer who'd cried, I needed to know the difference between what was real and what was a dream. I pinched myself to see if it hurt. By the time I let go there was a raised mark on my skin. I figured it was red. That was a good sign.

I was ready to get what I deserved.

II

IN CHAOS THEORY, DOES IT MATTER WHAT COLOR THE butterfly is? Would something entirely different have happened next if I hadn't been color-blind? Would Lazarus Jones have opened the door if the dress I'd worn was white, as I thought it was, rather than red, as it was in anyone else's eyes?

This is what he told me he saw from the upstairs window that first time I went to see him: A woman in a red dress standing on the porch. Out of place, out of time, steadily knocking on the door. Somebody who seemed intent on getting inside. He usually kept the shades drawn when people came looking for him. He had chased Dr. Wyman off with a gun, true enough. He wasn't interested in visitors. He didn't even talk to his own field-workers. But the red dress caught his eye. That's what he told me later. Maybe I reminded him of the fruit in his orchard on the day lightning struck. Something he hadn't expected and couldn't quite stop.

As for me, I was ready for anything. I thought I might explode, the way I had when I shoved my hand through the window. I told myself if he didn't come out of the house in five minutes, I would leave. Maybe I was indeed getting exactly what I deserved: nothing. A few minutes more and I probably would have been grateful for the opportunity to turn and run, the way I always had before. But I hadn't planned what I'd do next. Leave and do what? Drive off the Interstate into a canal? Jump from a cliff? Go home, lie down on the couch, look at the ceiling fan? All I knew is that I wanted to fly away. I wanted to be something brand-new. I felt like those human beings in fairy tales who suddenly find themselves in another creature's skin, trapped in sealskin, horsehide, feathers.

Lazarus Jones came out to the porch. I looked down at the ground. If he saw the expression on my face, I'd scare him off. Had I looked into a mirror, I would have frightened myself. I was desperate, you know. I was mired in death and wishes, trapped in the wrong skin. I was the donkey, ugly and braying, the goose girl asking for mercy, the beggarman in need of a crust of bread. The straps of my dress were falling off my shoulders. I didn't care. Dust was on my face and on my fingers. He'd had forty minutes of knowing everything; all I wanted was a little piece of what he'd learned on the other side. I didn't want to dissect him or photograph him or measure the radioactivity under his skin. I just wanted to be in the presence of a man it was impossible to kill.

There were birds overhead and I saw their shadows float by on the porch floorboards. It hurt to breathe. I should have apologized for intruding, or told him that I'd come a far distance only to ask how afraid I should be of death. I should have told him that the worst thing in the world is a wish that comes true. But I remained silent, the way I had so many times before.

"Who told you to come here?" he said.

What was I supposed to say? Fate? A butterfly on the other side of the world? The donkeyskin I wore, so itchy, so ill-fitting? An eight-year-old girl who breathed out one wish and changed everything?

"Are you trying to interview me, or something?" he wanted to know. He came over and took my arm. Did he test for lies this way? Could he feel a betrayal as easily as he could stop clocks?

His touch was so hot I almost fainted. But that might not have been about lightning.

"I'm just a librarian, not a reporter. From Orlon. I just wanted to see you for myself. They talked about you in my lightning group. They said you died and came back and now you're not afraid of anything. So why would you care whether or not I was here? You're not afraid, are you?"

Those were more words all strung together than I'd said in years. It was exhausting to talk. I felt as though I'd had to pull each word out of my throat, like stones I'd swallowed, with sharp edges.

Jones looked at me more carefully now that he understood I'd been struck. I wasn't just anyone, some busybody who had no idea of what he'd been through. He let go of my arm.

"If they say that about me, they're idiots. And if I wasn't afraid of anything I'd be one, too."

He was studying me, up and down. I felt too hot. I remembered I was in Florida. I remembered it would never snow here. I could be honest. To a point.

"My strike affected my left side," I said. "Nerve damage. Some cardiac damage as well. And I can't see the color red."

He laughed out loud; for a moment, his whole face changed.

"Is that funny?" I asked.

He stopped laughing. Stared at me. "Maybe."

"You're not going to pull a gun on me like you did to Dr. Wyman?"

"It wasn't loaded," Lazarus told me. "He ran before finding that out."

What no one had mentioned about Lazarus Jones was that he was beautiful. Younger than I was; twenty-five or thirty, I couldn't tell. His eyes were dark, darker than mine. I wondered if whatever he'd learned in those forty minutes had turned him to ash. He wore a long-sleeved white shirt and old jeans, work boots. His hair was dark and he hadn't had it cut in some time; it was longer than mine. When he stared there was something hot in his gaze, as though he could burn you alive if he wanted to. If you gave him a reason.

"Well, you're here," Lazarus said. "What do you want?"

This sounded like a trick question to me. If I answered incorrectly, perhaps I would turn into ash myself. Burned alive.

We stared at each other. Putting my hand through glass was nothing compared with this. I was in this moment, no other time. Now when I thought about New Jersey it was like remembering a mythological country.

You had to do the thing you were most afraid of, didn't you? In every fairy tale the right way was the difficult path, the one that led over boulders, through brambles, across a field of fire. I took a step forward and looped my arms around Lazarus Jones's neck so I could be near him. Every person had a secret, this was mine: I couldn't begin anything that remotely resembled a life until I understood death.

Lazarus Jones smelled like sulfur. People with sense run away from fire, but not me.

"Now that you've done it once, are you afraid to do it again?"

In response, he pulled me closer, just for an instant. For that time I didn't hear the clicking in my head, not one snap. I didn't smell oranges or feel the gritty dust.

"That's for me to know. I'm not sure you want to find out."

He let go and started walking away. Then he stopped and turned around. I was still there. He hadn't imagined me or gotten rid of me. Yet.

"You want to know what I'm afraid of?"

He cast a shadow along the yardspace between us. A dark shade. The sun was no longer blinding me. I could see right into his face. Maybe I nodded. I must have, because he spoke.

"It's the living that scares me most of all," Lazarus Jones said.

He went on then, inside his house. After he'd closed the door, I heard the lock click into place. I felt lost, standing there. Sweltering in the sun. It was so hot out no birds were in the sky. They were all perched in the shadows.

A group of men were sitting in the shade as well, taking a break from picking oranges. One of them approached me as I walked back to my car. He was young, high-school age, tall and rangy. He had a curious, friendly expression and his hair was buzzed off. He reminded me of Renny, but he was healthy and strong; his hands were rough, covered with blisters. I wondered if the blisters caused him great pain. If he rubbed them with Vaseline. If some girl who loved him put his fingers in her mouth, healed him with a kiss.

"Was that Jones you were talking to?" the boy asked me.

"For a minute," I said.

"He never talks to any of us. He leaves what we're owed out on the porch. Then the fruit distributor sends trucks out, and those guys have nothing to do with him, either. I never even saw him before today. You were up close. Was he all deformed, or something?"

Deformed, no. Merely beautiful. But I didn't think it was my place to comment if Jones wanted to keep himself locked away.

"I couldn't really tell."

"That's what we all figure. He got hit by lightning and he's all scarred up."

"I didn't see anything."

"Let us know if you find out. Maybe we're all working for a fucking monster." The boy laughed at that notion. "Maybe he's a bloodsucking creature from beyond the grave."

"He wasn't," I said. Just beautiful, filled with ashes, shutting the door in my face. Only that.

"But you couldn't really tell," the boy challenged me. "Could you?" The other guys were whistling for him, calling his name, so he headed back to them. "See ya," he called as he ambled back into the shade.

I got into my car and took off, but I was rattled. I pulled onto the Interstate going the wrong way and didn't realize my mistake until I'd driven north for three exits. Orlon was to the south. Finally, I turned around and pulled off at a rest stop. I used the toilet and bought a bottle of water. The cashier complimented me on my red dress and then I realized why Lazarus Jones had laughed at my color blindness. I understood why the men in the gas station where I'd stopped before had whistled. They thought they knew who I was because of my red dress. I felt hot and confused; where he'd grabbed my arm heat blisters had risen. Where he'd whispered to me, my ear was burning.

I went home, took off my dress, and hung it in the back of the closet. The next morning, when I went out to my car, I noticed that the odometer had stopped. I wondered if the malfunction had been brought on by proximity to Lazarus Jones. There was something wrong with me as well. Definitely caused by Lazarus. Wherever he had touched me I had little raised burn marks. I went to the Orlon University Health Center, to see the nurse who'd examined me for the lightning-strike study. He name was June Malone and she was a year or two younger than I.

"You've missed a couple of meetings," she said.

"Have I?" Like I was ever going again. "These things actually hurt." I showed her my arm.

June gave me an ointment for my skin, but she seemed suspicious. Maybe it looked as though I'd mutilated myself, held a hot match to my flesh.

"I'm sensitive," I told her.

"So I see."

"Seriously, the slightest thing affects me," I assured her.

"We need to report this to the study. Any new effect can be meaningful."

"Look, I'm not the type to be in a study. And don't these studies benefit the clinicians and the scientists, not the patients?"

I did agree to revisit the cardiologist, a fellow named Craven, who was in charge of my case but never seemed to recognize me. Thankfully, though, he recognized my heart. I suppose that was the important thing. I'd had a new electro-cardiogram and Craven studied the results. He asked if my heart was racing. I admitted it was. I was given a prescription for nitroglycerin and told that when my heart started hurting I should slip a tablet under my tongue. I might occasionally experience angina brought on by the neurological and cardiac shock of the strike. Very common. I limped out of there with my ointment and my nitro, a commonplace wreck.

I spied Renny as I was walking across the campus. It was the first week of summer school and he was taking Modern

Architecture; that was his major. In all honesty I wanted to avoid him; I didn't want a friend. But he spotted me and shouted out for me to wait, so I did.

"Trying to sneak away?" Renny was wearing khaki shorts, sneakers, an Orlon University T-shirt, and his heavy leather gloves.

"I was being treated for a disgusting little skin condition." I showed him my arm. We sat down on a bench under a cabbage palm.

"Want to trade?" he said. When he saw the look on my face he added, "I'm kidding. Just a little levity. No guilt if my effects are worse than yours. We're beyond that. Fellow survivors and all."

I suppose as friends we suited each other in some strange way. He told me a little about his life — his parents were doctors in Miami, his younger sister was still in high school. The only thing he'd ever been interested in was building things; he'd been obsessed with architecture since the first time he played with blocks. Now with his hands afflicted, he worried that architecture might no longer be an option.

Renny was only twenty-one, but he seemed older once he got to talking. He gazed at the other students passing by. I saw what was in his eyes. The others had no idea of what he'd been through. They were moving through a world in which people didn't limp or have holes in their heads. In their universe no one wore gloves when the temperature climbed toward a hundred degrees. No one woke in the middle of the night, in pain, alone. A stranger in his own life.

"Do you think every person has one defining secret?" Renny asked.

I laughed, nursing my own most current secret, Lazarus Jones. "Don't you think we're more complex than that? Don't we all have endless secrets?"

"Little, bullshit ones. Sure. I don't mean those. Who do you love? Who did you fuck? Everyone has them. I mean one defining secret. The essence of a person. If you figure that out, you figure out the riddle of that particular human being."

"Is this your way of getting me to confide in you?"

"Maybe. Just give me one of your bullshit secrets. But be careful. That might make us friends."

I was surprised. Though he was a stranger to me, I'd thought he had assumed we were friends. Renny, it turned out, wasn't easy to fool. I suppose he was used to people shrugging him off. The sun was in his face, blurring his features. All in all, Renny wasn't a bad-looking guy, but not a single girl walking by had glanced at him. The limp, the withered foot, the hole in his head, the gloves. That's what they saw.

Would it hurt me to give him something? Just a tiny bit?

"I went to see Lazarus Jones."

Renny stared at me, then threw his head back and laughed. He might have even chortled. "Now that is bullshit."

"Seriously. I did."

"Bullshit and crap. Times two."

"Fine. Don't believe me."

"Yeah, well then, tell me. Did he really chase Wyman off with a gun?"

"Unloaded. He didn't want to be their lab rat."

"Wow. Sympathy for the devil. Maybe you really did meet him."

"He's not the devil. And I'm hardly sympathetic." Now that was bullshit. "He owns an orange grove." Enough of this. "Okay, so now give me one of your secrets."

"There's one," Renny said mournfully.

I followed his gaze. Several young women were on their way to the dorms. Frankly, I couldn't tell one from the other. They were all pretty and young.

"The one on the left."

The blonde.

"Iris McGinnis. She was in my art history class in the spring. She doesn't know I'm alive. I'm insanely crazy about her."

"This isn't your defining secret, is it?"

Instead of answering, Renny said, "Look at her. No one will ever be in love with me."

"You're not the only one in the world with a terrible love life. I'm right there with you."

There was no need for him to know about the policeman in the parking lot or my friends' boyfriends in high school or the fact that I liked the way the burns on my arms felt, what they reminded me of. Sitting there with Renny, I wondered if choosing the red dress had been an accident. Was there a part of my brain that could still sense red, just as it sensed desire?

When Renny went to class I walked to my car and headed for the library. I had decided to get the library records in

order. It was the least I could do to make up for all my ab-
sences. I was taking Frances's handwritten notations and en-
tering them into the word processor. On each patron's card
Frances had painstakingly recorded every book he or she
had checked out. There was one woman, for instance, who
had withdrawn every book on architecture that we had,
then had ordered more. I wondered if she'd be a possibility
for Renny until I came to her birth date and discovered this
particular patron was nearly eighty years old. No match, I
supposed, for the beautiful Iris McGinnis.

It was a Thursday afternoon, and as I worked I couldn't
help but overhear the preschool reading group. Frances was
reading Andersen's "Everything in Its Right Place," in
which the pious heroine is nothing like the Goose Girl in the
Grimms' tale. There were no heads nailed to the wall in this
story. No cases of mistaken identity that weren't easily recti-
fied. A few of the mothers eyed me. I suppose there might be
toddlers who continued to have nightmares from my time in
command of story hour. No wonder their mothers wanted
me kept at a distance. If I spoke, anything at all might drop
from my lips: blood, frogs, death wishes, desire.

I kept to my files. I was in the A's all afternoon. Before
long my brother's name came up. I hadn't seen him in
weeks; now it was as though I had stumbled upon him, face-
to-face. I was surprised Ned had ever been to this library,
when the university facility was so superior. The science li-
brary in the north quad ranked alongside the University of
Miami's collection, the result of a major donation by an
Orlon alum who had invented a plastic attachment for fail-

ing kidneys. But my brother indeed had a library card here, and as it turned out, he had used it. I slipped his card into my backpack to look at later on.

When I went home, the wind had risen. A hot wind. I parked and got out. I had the sense of being lost that I often had here, as though I'd been transported to Florida by means I didn't understand. I'd blinked and my life had disappeared. There was Giselle, sitting in the weeds, her tail flashing back and forth. My familiar. She followed me in the door, and when I sat down on the couch, she leapt up and stared at me. The wind came through the screens and made the ceiling fan spin, though it was turned off. I took out my brother's library card and Giselle tapped at it with her paw.

Knock, knock. Who's there?

I couldn't imagine my brother reading anything but scientific journals and texts. Yet he had withdrawn the complete Grimm's fairy tales not once, but twice. He'd actually had to pay an overdue fine. What would he have done with such stories? Why on earth had he wanted them? I'd had to force him to read them to me when we were children. *Please, this one. That one. Not one about Death.* He'd always had some comment to make: Genetically impossible for men to turn into beasts. Ridiculous to imagine that a woman could sleep for a hundred years. Absurd to think the dead could speak in rhymes and the living could make wishes that came true. But the logic of fairy tales was that there was no logic: bad things happened to the innocent, children were set out in the woods by their parents, fear walked hand in hand with experience, a wish spoken aloud could make it so.

I fed the cat, then took a cold bath. The blisters were still on my skin. To me they looked like flecks of snow. I shivered in my tub of water and watched the light fade. I had gone to Lazarus Jones because I thought he could help me understand what had happened on that January day when I was a child. Her very last moments, that's what I was interested in. Did a person's life flash before her eyes, all she'd had and all she'd lost? Or was it the last few instants that mattered most of all? Did the immediate past last forever, a tape that kept playing somewhere in the universe? Was the last thing my mother saw a sheet of ice? Was she listening to the radio, singing along? I suppose what I really wanted to know was if she despised me for the wish I'd made, whether it was possible in any way, in any world, for her to ever forgive me.

I let the water in the bath drain, and after I dressed I went outside. It was still hot. Too hot to breathe. The wind rattled, knocked things about. The palm fronds smacked against one another. Giselle followed me out and went to sit beside the hedge, waiting for the moles that sometimes wandered onto our lawn. I wondered if this would ever feel like home. If anything ever would. I wondered if this book was my brother's defining secret, or just a small part of who he truly was.

Far away, there was thunder, a common enough occurrence in Florida, something most people ignored. I thought of Ned surrounded by a whirlwind, like the nucleus of an atom, trapped within itself. I thought of him walking into the Orlon Public Library looking for answers, still trying to understand what we did wrong. I wanted to telephone my brother and say, *Tell me the truth. Do you believe a wish can kill? Do you believe we could have changed something that night, stopped the ice from falling, stopped our mother from getting in her car? If we'd run along the road till she turned around, woken from sleep and called the police with a premonition, would she still be alive? Tell me, brother, could we have done anything differently, you and I?*

Fire

I

WHAT IS THE DIFFERENCE BETWEEN LOVE AND obsession? Didn't both make you stay up all night, wandering the streets, a victim of your own imagination, your own heartbeat? Didn't you fall into both, headfirst into quicksand? Wasn't every man in love a fool and every woman a slave?

Love was like rain: it turned to ice, or it disappeared. Now you saw it, now you couldn't find it no matter how hard you might search. Love evaporated; obsession was realer; it hurt, like a pin in your bottom, a stone in your shoe. It didn't go away in the blink of an eye. A morning phone call filled with regret. A letter that said, *Dear you, good-bye from me*. Obsession tasted like something familiar. Something you'd known your whole life. It settled and lurked; it stayed with you.

I tried to define what was happening to me. I had decided never again to drive out to the Jones orchard, and yet I could see the map that led there simply by closing my eyes. I often had lunch with Renny in the school cafeteria, but despite the salad in front of me, all I could taste was an orange, the sweet kind with the reddish rind, the sort that to me looked like ice. My mouth puckered. My heart raced. I thought of all those silly lovelorn girls I'd known in high school, and for once felt a bit of compassion. Foolish creatures. Foolish me. At night I dreamed of things that were dangerous: snakes, stepladders, horses' heads nailed to the wall. When it rained I stood by the window, looking for lightning. There were music students who lived down the street and when they practiced in the evenings, the sound of the oboe made me weep, the piano forced me to cover my ears. I suppose I had begun to feel something, just an itch. Just a sting. That was the problem. I was such a novice I didn't understand what it meant when I couldn't sleep, couldn't eat, when my racing thoughts were too often of Lazarus Jones.

Since I didn't believe in love, I soon enough defined my state as a delusionary preoccupation. Obsession. An emotion that should be tied up and taken out with the trash, replaced by more serious, less affecting thoughts. I turned to work, or what little there was of it at the library. But even there my obsessive nature took over. I pretended to be cheerfully busy, entering information into the computer, dusting and ordering the shelves, but in fact my new, rather prurient interest was looking up people's reading habits. It was disgusting, really. An invasion of privacy, a petty crime of the soul. I'd begun by looking up my brother's card; now I couldn't seem to stop. That was my nature, to take something bad and make it worse.

I looked up which novels my physical therapist most enjoyed, thick nineteenth-century tomes in which problems weren't easily solved with exercise and diet. I saw that Matt Acres, owner of the hardware store, preferred biographies of adventurers, men who left behind their safe and settled lives. Dr. Wyman's teenaged daughter, who was home for the summer from private school in New England, had read all of D. H. Lawrence. People in the Orlon Home for the Aged most often requested travel books for places they would surely never see: Egypt, Paris, Venice, Mexico. My mailman was reading poetry; no wonder what little mail I received was crumpled and stained. The griddle cook at the diner, who made a terrible omelet and even worse blueberry pancakes, read Kafka, in German.

If Frances York had known what I was doing, I would have been fired on the spot. What people read revealed so much about them that she considered our card catalog a treasure house of privileged secrets; each card contained the map of an individual's soul. I knew Frances's philosophy. It was not our job to monitor the books our patrons withdrew any more than it was our duty to alter their reading habits. I liked Frances and respected her, but I wondered if she would have hired me in the first place had she known who I really was. I was poison long before I'd started snooping around. Would she have felt safe with a person who knew more about the effects of arsenic than she did about the Dewey decimal system? A death addict and a thief who didn't know wrong from right, white from red? At least now I'd had Peggy come by to help color-code my clothes; I knew enough to wear white blouses and black skirts to work and to leave my red clothes at home. But I was still me, hidden by sensible shoes, by skirts past my knee and button-down blouses.

Thankfully, Frances had no reason to suspect any of this. I was a model employee: polite to our patrons, cheerfully running books out to those who were housebound or in the hospital. I even made a weekly trip to the home for the aged with a box of travel books. Could anyone have discerned I was not to be trusted? Not for a second. Well, maybe those mothers from the nursery group, they seemed to know, but I wasn't counting them. I avoided the children's section as a matter of fact. The bright illustrations, the rhymes, the high hopes, all made me nervous. Child patrons always wanted something: directions to the bathroom, a drink of water, a sequel to a book that doesn't have one.

The children's section was where the tall windows were, and the sunlight filtering through in pale streams revealed how filthy the shelves were. There were dust motes everywhere. I ventured into that section one morning with a mop and a sponge. At least it was a school day, and there were no children around. Only me.

By accident, I found the book my brother had taken out.

Or perhaps there were no accidents; perhaps I saw the book out of the corner of my eye, and my brain processed the discovery in some deep place I couldn't reach. However it happened, I turned and there it was, not put back properly, askew on the shelf. It was an old edition of Grimm's, black with silver lettering. The pages smelled watery; when I held the book up to my nose I sneezed. Tears in my eyes. So what? I just happened to pick it up. I just happened to sit on the floor cross-legged and thumb through the pages.

One story in particular had clearly been a favorite, perhaps of my brother, with dog-eared pages and a coffee stain or two. It was "Godfather Death," one of the stories I'd hated and had always passed by. In this tale, whenever Death stands at the feet of an ill person, that person belongs to him. To trick Death, a good doctor, the kind hero, turns the ill person around so that Death is at the head and therefore cannot take him. Fairy-tale logic can be intractable or fluid, and the hero never knows which it is. Especially if the hero is a rational man. This one is.

One more time and I'll take you instead, Death says, but the doctor is a scientist through to his soul, a believer in order and in the rightness of things; he cannot accept this is the way the game of life and death is played. There have to be rules, and he is convinced that all he needs is to reverse Death's direction. But when the doctor saves the girl he loves by turning her around to avoid her fate, Death scoops him up instead. Then and there. No explanations, just a single final act. A life for a life.

Is this the way the story ends? Not in Andersen's tales surely, where right and might win out, but this is Grimm.

There is a single, simple rule to the game played between the doctor and Death, one the doctor-hero has ignored: When it comes to death, heads or tails matters not. There is no escape in the end.

It's a sad tale, one that defies logic and thumbs its nose at any reasonable man's attempt to impose order on the natural world. That my brother, of all people, would choose this obscure, dark story to read and reread was in itself a puzzle. I thought about the way he'd called to me when I'd stood out on the porch, watching our mother drive away. Turn around, that's what he'd wanted me to do. If I had, would Death have passed us by?

Just when I thought my brother was determined to avoid me — I'd hardly seen him since my strike — he and Nina invited me to their house for a party. I'd been so taken aback when Ned called that I'd said *yes* when in fact I'd meant *no*. I couldn't remember the last time I'd been to a party outside of events at the library in New Jersey, and I'd arranged all of them. I'd come to realize that I was comfortable speaking only to people who'd experienced disaster, at least in a secondhand way, like my physical therapist, Peggy, whom I occasionally met for coffee. And of course Renny, not that he was a friend, not even close. Now I'd gone and committed myself to a party of mathematicians and scientists.

It turned out to be an annual event, filled with professors and graduate students from both Nina's and Ned's departments. Getting there was a trial for me; I took one wrong turn after another on those curlicue roads that cut through the campus and all looked alike. I realized then, I hadn't once been invited over to my brother's house since my arrival in Florida, and I thought this strange. I wondered if my sister-in-law held something against me. Or maybe it was Ned.

The house my brother and Nina owned was modern, glass and stucco, set on a cul-de-sac on the far side of the Orlon campus — faculty housing of the highest quality. No wonder some of the best minds chose to teach at Orlon; life here was pleasant, a fact that rubbed me the wrong way. I could feel the numbness in my fingertips, the clicking in my head when I pulled up to park. In times of stress, my symptoms intensified. I got out of my car and walked up the neat path. Nice lawn. Nice flowers. I was thinking about Lazarus Jones. I shouldn't have been, but after a week I was still burning. I could see happy graduate students through the bay window of Nina and Ned's house. I felt as though I had arrived from an alternate universe. Call it New Jersey, call it desperation, call it whatever you like.

I went immediately to the bar set up in the den. I poured a large glass of red wine for myself, probably the good stuff. It looked like mud to me. While I was getting myself a drink, and then another, I could tell how devoted my brother's students were to him; I overheard one say that Ned would be the head of the department when Dr. Miller, the current chair, retired. Several voiced their disappointment that Ned would be taking the next semester off from teaching, something I didn't know, in order to concentrate on his research.

Nina's students were more reserved, until they started in on the wine; then they were wild. They had a slew of drinking games with mathematical rules I couldn't understand. They also seemed devoted, only more quietly so; I could see into the kitchen, where they had gathered around Nina as she dished out bouillabaisse, homemade, I was told, which shocked me. I had assumed someone as theoretical and removed as Nina wouldn't know how to cook. But, of course, cuisine was probably just another equation to her: clams to tomato sauce, basil to pepper, rum to lemonade. My previous apathy toward my sister-in-law had turned into hostility. Why hadn't she invited me here before, made her bouillabaisse for me? Perhaps she saw me as another project of my brother's, one of many that took up time and energy with little or no return for his efforts.

I stayed out of the kitchen and close to the bar. One graduate student in meteorology took a fancy to me. He introduced himself and followed me around for a while. I was wearing the red dress again, that must have been it. The graduate student, Paul, had heard about my lightning strike and wanted to talk about my effects. Was I dizzy? Weak in the knees? Did I have migraine headaches? Lasting psychological effects? Would I like a bowl of bouillabaisse, a glass of punch? How was sex affected, this was what he yearned to know. Hotter? Colder? There was the myth of hypersexuality, duly noted, half believed. Would the rearrangement of my electrical impulses take my partner's breath away, bring him closer to the brink of the world we knew?

This was a little too personal. I thought we'd speak of the weather, the heat, perhaps the student's classwork, not the edge of the known world. I spied my brother across the room. I almost didn't recognize him. He looked older, unkempt, thinner. Had I not noticed that he'd lost most of his hair, that his shoulders slumped? Yet he seemed to be enjoying himself. He was talking with several other professors, laughing at someone's joke. I wondered if he'd found happiness in logic, in this well-ordered world created from scratch in a land where there was no ice. Perhaps Death stood outside the windows in Orlon. Perhaps he couldn't get through the glass.

I excused myself and left the graduate student to his own kind. The bar had only beer and wine, and I needed something stronger to get through the evening. I went into the kitchen, found the liquor cabinet, and poured myself a whiskey. My grandmother had liked whiskey now and then, and I had sometimes joined her in a drink. Tea and whiskey, our cocktail of choice. We liked to sit in the parlor and watch snow fall; we played "I spy with my little eye" long after her vision was failing and I was far too old for such games. Now I raised my glass and drank to my grandmother's memory. Someone who had loved me in spite of everything, no matter who and what I was.

It was because of the way I missed my grandmother that I drank the whiskey so fast, then turned to the window when I did. It was because I was a failure in each and every thing I undertook, including being a guest at a dinner party, that I happened to spy someone standing in the grass. Was that chaos theory, or simply chaos? If an ice age could be triggered by trivial shifts in the earth's orbit, what might be wrought by a woman in tears? It was dark in the yard, and at first I thought I was seeing a statue. She was wearing a white dress, and she wasn't moving. But it was Nina, my brother's wife, the mathematician, weeping.

After a moment, Nina saw me through the glass. I think

she opened her mouth. She was gulping down air, in a panic. I thought of Death, unable to take those who were turned from him. I did exactly that. I quickly turned my back to her. Perhaps I could pretend I hadn't seen her. Perhaps she could pretend as well. Wasn't that the way most people went about their lives? Put it in a box, tie it up tight, walk away. Please, oh please, let's do.

In the living room the students were devouring the refreshments. Who would have expected them to be so hungry? French bread, cheeses, white snowy berries that were most likely strawberries, punch, champagne, plenty of beer. The guests were cheerful — not gloomy and serious, as I had expected. Weren't they all researching the end of the known universe, the end of the numerical continuum, continually trying to make sense out of columns of figures that refused to cooperate? Shouldn't these students be glum, desperate? Shouldn't they realize what little sense there was to be made of this world?

"Your brother always gives the best parties," someone said to me. I suppose that was a compliment. I found it surreal. I had never seen my brother speak at length to another person besides Nina and the funeral director in New Jersey when we were planning my grandmother's funeral. Pine box, small gathering, white flowers that looked like a snowbank. I hadn't known this part of him, just as I hadn't know of his interest in fairy tales.

"You're leaving?" Ned caught up to me as I headed for the front door.

Perhaps I'd never known him, and only thought I had. "Lovely party, but I don't belong here. Look at them all.

I barely speak their language. Math and science. I do not fit in."

"Library science," my brother reminded me.

We both laughed. Had we ever done that before?

"Well, you seem much improved." Ned sounded hopeful. I hated when he did that.

"Seems that way."

My brother looked at me carefully. "Meaning?"

I wanted to say, meaning Death is not standing at my feet, not at the moment at any rate, not right now. I was thinking about the volume of fairy tales on the shelf. I wanted to ask Ned what else there was I didn't know about him. Instead, I said, "Meaning yes. Sure. I'm improved. But you look like crap."

My brother ran a hand through what was left of his hair.

"Probably a gift from our father. Baldness."

"I think you inherit that gene from your mother. You look skinny, too. Maybe you're the one who should go to the doctor."

"I have to say, I'm glad you came to the party." My brother seemed genuinely happy I was there. "I know you don't like these kinds of gatherings."

"I didn't want to be rude."

"Really? That never stopped you before."

I could see through the crowd into the kitchen. Nina was back. She had shaken off whatever had possessed her in the garden and was now serving punch to the students.

"Thank Nina for me, will you?"

"Will do." My brother looked behind him. Nina waved to him across the room. "Lucky me," he said, and waved back.

I drove home, if that's what my rented cottage could be called. I let the cat out and drank a tall glass of whiskey and fell asleep on the couch. The quiet was overwhelming. I liked to be alone, or so I'd always thought. I fell asleep quickly; I was drunk, I suppose, exhausted in some deep way. I dreamed that my sister-in-law was a butterfly. I dreamed my grandmother was sweeping the floor. I dreamed I reached into a dark bucket of water and felt fish swim through my fingers; the coldness of that water turned to heat and rose up my arms, through my bloodstream, up to my chest.

There was a knock on my door, and in my dreams I turned from the bucket too quickly and tipped it over. Water spilled on the floor, one drop at a time. Clear and then white and then red. That's the way truth always surfaces in fairy tales, written in glass, in snow, in blood. As I came to consciousness I had a feeling of dread, the way I had on the morning after my mother's accident. You can be betrayed in your sleep. The whole world can tilt while you're dreaming of butterflies.

I was still in the confines of my dreamworld as I went to the door. Rats, cats, bats, any of them might find their way up the path. I felt true panic. It was a feeling I remembered wholly. *Go back to bed, it's too dark, it's too icy, it's too late.*

I was relieved to find that my caller was only a delivery-man, bringing me a cardboard box of flowers. I laughed and had him wait while I went to find my purse. I tipped him ten dollars, extravagant for me.

Giselle came running in, something in her mouth.

"You've got a little hunter," the deliveryman declared.

"Oh, lovely."

Two little paws hung out of the cat's jaws.

A murderess. The perfect pet for me.

A trail of blood dripped onto the floor as the cat trotted by. I couldn't see the color, but I remembered it. I had hoped to see the feathers of some nasty crow or the whiskers of a rat, but instead Giselle dropped one of the moles she was always waiting for beside the hedges. Blind, and soft as a glove, helpless. Caught at last.

Before I went over to deal with the mess, I lifted the cover of the box of flowers. Roses. Right away, I called to the deliveryman to ask what color they were.

He laughed, then saw I was serious.

"Color-blind," I explained.

The deliveryman was young and apologetic. "Sorry, I thought you were kidding. They're red."

But they were white to me, as my admirer knew they would be. The duality of the gift amused me, but it also frightened me. One visit and Lazarus Jones thought he knew me. Fairy tales are riddles, and people are riddles, too. Figure one out and he's yours forever, whether he likes it or not.

Giselle was hovering over her prey in a corner; I shooed her away with a newspaper.

"Go on! Leave it alone!"

The cat had played her part, but the game seemed all wrong. The mole was curled up like a leaf. I sat down and when the poor little thing didn't move, I picked it up with a bit of newspaper. The mole was lifeless. All the same, I held it up to my ear, the way some people do with shells to hear a far-off sea.

After a while I got a shoebox from the closet, filled it with tissues, and lay the mole's body inside. When I had time I would bury it next to the hedge, where it belonged. Now I was busy cleaning the blood off the floor, a trail that looked like snow to me.

Giselle had figured out the riddle of the mole: stay beside the hedge long enough, it will appear and be yours. Blind and gentle, plodding through the dark, unable to see stars or teeth, it assumes what is safe one day will be safe again the next. That was how you caught somebody, easy as pie, in one bite. That was how I'd been caught, too. I put the roses in the freezer overnight. Cold storage for a cold heart. I didn't know if I wanted them or not. In the morning, when I took them out from between the ice cubes and the cans of frozen juice, the roses shimmered. That's all someone in the grip of an obsession needs: the single possibility that desire might be real, a tiny shred of evidence to show you're not all alone in the dark. I thought of poor Jack Lyons, offering me field flowers in the parking lot in New Jersey. I thought of Jack far too often as a matter of fact. All the same, he hadn't a clue as to who I was. But these roses sent by Lazarus Jones were so sharp a person could cut herself and draw blood. That was the key to my riddle. For all I'd done, for all I'd wished, a rose made of ice was exactly what I deserved.

I DROVE OUT IN THE MORNING, WHEN THE SKY WAS STILL dark and the rising heat pressed down on the earth. There was rain in the forecast, and I could feel the change in the atmosphere inside my body. In the night I'd dreamed I had long dark hair. There was ice all over my body. I was so cold in my dream that I woke up shivering. Now in the brutal temperature of the hazy morning I stopped at a service station, bought a diet Coke and gassed up my car. I crunched on ice. There was the smell of oil and oranges and heat. I'd been more careful about my clothes this time: A black T-shirt, jeans, sandals, nothing that would make anyone stare. It took me close to an hour to get to the orchard on this occasion, time enough to change my mind. I wasn't thinking much. I wasn't seriously hoping for anything. I had the radio on and before I knew it I was listening to Johnny Cash. I thought of the roofer who'd been struck while doing penance for the affair he'd been having; he should have known he was done for when he heard "Ring of Fire." And here it was again, playing on the AM station I was tuned to. People played that song a lot around Orlon. They listened to the warning, then walked right into the burning ring, clear-headed and stupid at the same time.

I had all the windows open and the sky was getting light. If I were to have an accident now, the last thing I'd hear would be Johnny Cash's voice. Would I hear it forever, the deep dark sound of it, all that pain bundled up inside? I was eight years older than my mother had been at the time when it happened, her age and mine combined. Now when I thought of her she seemed so young, almost as though she were the daughter, gone off to a celebration on a January night, her pale hair freshly washed, her hopeful blue scarf, ready for life. I was the little old lady left on the porch, the witch stomping her feet on the ice.

When I got to the orchard I parked and got out, then reached into the backseat. I'd brought the frozen bouquet of flowers with me, packed with ice in a plastic bag. It was a test, of course. I was anxious to see how he'd do. Did he really know me, or had the choice of red roses been pure chance?

It was still early but Lazarus Jones was awake. He'd heard the car, peered out the window, opened the door, and now stood looking out. The door was half open, half shut. The paint was peeling off the porch railings. Out in the field there were half a dozen men working. A few looked over in our direction, but I doubted they could see anything. The sunlight, after all, was blinding. It made sunspots appear in front of your eyes.

Lazarus was wearing old jeans and a button-down blue shirt; his hair was wet from a shower. It was broiling hot already. I thought I had never seen such a beautiful man in all my life. Everything seemed unreal — the white oranges, the sound of trucks in the fields, the way he was looking at me.

"I guess I have a visitor," he said.

"You must have wanted one. I figured this was an invitation." I held out the flowers, ice covering the petals, stems black with cold. "I never got roses from anyone."

He opened the screen door wider. "I guess I passed the test," he said. "I knew what you wanted."

He wasn't the kind of man I would ever end up with. He was the sort some gorgeous woman snagged for her own; perhaps they'd been high school sweethearts, they'd been true to each other since the day they'd met. Two beautiful people, meant for each other. My left side was crooked, my hair patchy, my skin blotchy; I was ten years too old for him. But I was here at the door. I was the one he'd sent roses to.

We went into the house and stood in the front hall. There was an umbrella stand and a rack laden with jackets and hats. There was a wooden bench where a person could sit and pull on his boots. The hallway was dark, dusty. Everything was. The windows hadn't been cleaned in a long time. Once you were in the house you couldn't tell what the weather was outside. It had its own atmosphere, apart from the rest of the world. There was a dull thrumming, an evenness, almost a deadness to the air, which I guessed might have been caused by Lazarus. The survivors in my group swore he could affect almost anything.

Why did I stay? Because for once there was something louder than the continuous clicking in my head. Because he'd opened the door. I was startled by how consumed with desire I was. I was thinking the kind of thoughts I hadn't had before. So this was it. The thing that made people do stupid, ridiculous things; this was everything, here in the dark hall.

We went on into the kitchen. His breakfast was on the table: a glass of ice water, a bowl of cold cereal, a napkin, a spoon. I realized the flowers were melting, so I put them in the sink.

"The worst of my effects is my inability to see red. I miss it and I never even liked it. Just my luck."

"You have bad luck? I'll bet there's more wrong with me than there is with you." Lazarus held his hand over the spoon on the table. It lurched forward. Spun in a circle. When it stopped there was a clanging noise.

"That's a trick," I said.

"Electromagnetic something or other. Let's just say it's a disorder."

"What else can you do?"

My stomach was lurching around. I was falling into something. Hard. If I stayed, my bones would shatter; I'd break into pieces at his feet. Stupid girl. Stupid me. I hadn't turned to ice for nothing, for this, a stranger who wasn't right for me in any way. It would take minutes to run down the hall and get into my car; driving over the speed limit, I could be back in Orlon in under an hour. But I already knew I wasn't going anywhere.

"You think I'm a magician?" He said it with contempt. As though he was used to having people look down on him, ready and waiting for that.

I tilted my chin up. Faced him straight on. "Maybe."

"You have some children you want me to entertain at a birthday party — is that it? Me and a pony and some rabbits. You'd have to pay and I'm not cheap."

"I don't like children," I said.

He laughed, surprised.

"And I don't have anyone."

He understood. There was no one in my life.

"Then I'll just entertain you."

He went to the table and picked up a napkin. For an instant I thought he was about to show me a party trick. Just to get back at me. Out of pride. A rabbit made out of paper; a toy bird that would spin and flutter in the air. Instead, he held the paper to his mouth and breathed out.

The faucet in the sink dripped; the sound overpowered

the clicking in my head. I watched as the paper ignited. The flame was so hot it was blue. When it rose too high and his fingers were being singed, Lazarus let the burning paper fall into the bowl of cereal, where it burned to ash. I'd never known fire had a sound, like a gasp, a sigh, something alive.

"Do you have anything that can beat that?" he said.

I could make a wish and turn it into blood and bones. What was that worth? I had ice in my veins; I was colder and more distant than a dark, sunless planet. If that's what he wanted, then I might just be the perfect woman for him. I went to the table and took the glass of ice water. I filled my mouth with ice. A woman who stood in one place, who forever looked at the sky, motionless, frozen solid. If that's what he wanted, that's what he'd get. I kissed him, mouth open. I could feel the heat from inside him melting through, but I kept at it. It was why I was here, I knew that now. I couldn't stop kissing him. I heard myself, my desire, and I couldn't believe it was me. I was moaning. I sounded like the fire had, a gasp, a sigh. The riddle inside me: How do you melt ice? How can you move when you're frozen inside?

When the ice cubes inside my mouth had turned to water, and the water was nearly boiling, I pulled away. I went to the sink to spit out before I burned myself. Quite suddenly I knew what the myth of people struck by lightning becoming more sexual was made of. It was simply this: We knew we could be gone at any time. Standing by the window, up on the roof, playing golf, on the phone. The possibility of being blown out like a match made us burn.

"Well." Lazarus looked surprised at what he'd wound up with. "You do have some tricks."

I was drawn to him, a sparrow to a hawk, a hawk to a sparrow. There was no logic when I followed him down the hall to the bathroom. There was no reason for me to do the things I did. Except that I felt something. I didn't think that was possible for me anymore. Not now, not ever. That I did seemed enough to excuse almost anything.

He filled the tub with water. All I could hear was the sound of the tap. I understood that it was the only way we could be together — the elements most drawn to each other are the ones that destroy each other. I leaned down and put one hand in the tub, splashed back and forth. The water felt like ice. I could feel it down my spine. Lazarus said it was nothing compared with the bath of ice they'd put him in at the hospital, when he was burning up alive and they needed to lower his temperature, keep his heart going. It had probably kept him alive. Pure ice. Now he craved it. A cold woman like me. I think he'd been dreaming of me and then I was there, in my red dress.

The day was humid and now it started to rain. We could hear the rain hitting against the roof. There was thunder. I could be anywhere. I couldn't leave.

"I need it to be dark," Lazarus told me.

I didn't care. I wanted whatever he did. He drew the blinds over the window, shut off the light above the sink. We could barely see each other. Then the last light. That one out, too. We were in the dark, groping, following our hands, hearts, skin. In truth, I was grateful for the dark. I wasn't beautiful. I couldn't forget that I was ten years older than he. I slipped off my clothes, stepped into the tub, shuddered in the cold water. He got in right after me, desperate, I think, wanting me; it must have been that. I could feel the edges of heat in the water. I held on to the smooth sides of the bathtub. I thought of fish in a bucket. Death standing at the foot of a bed. When he pulled himself on top of me, I imagined I might drown. Maybe I was supposed to. For all I knew, this was the other half of my death wish — half fire, half water. He drew me under and kissed me, deep, underwater, unending. By the time we came up for air, I was burning. I turned on the cold tap and let it run. Over my shoulders, over my chest, in the dark that I was grateful for. I could have been anywhere, but I was there. I could have driven west or east, but I had driven here to him. I closed my eyes. *Burn me. Drown me. Do anything.* When he moved inside, I pulled him deeper.

When I got out of the bathtub my legs were shaking. Water had spilled onto the floor. Every step was slippery, dangerous, cold. "I have to do something," I said.

I wrapped a towel around me, then went to the kitchen to open the freezer. My hands were shaking. This was really crazy. I got a piece of ice and pushed it up inside me, where I was burning. I didn't care. It was worth it. I wasn't sure I had ever felt anything before.

"I hurt you," Lazarus said.

He had pulled on his clothes and come up behind me. Nothing had hurt me since that night on the porch; nothing had even come close. I was shaking, still wet, so he put his arms around me. I could feel the heat through his clothes. I could hear his heart beating, the strong heart that had defied death, that had stopped and come back to life. Nothing could have made me want him more.

I wasn't much different than that greedy, selfish girl I'd been years ago. Only now I didn't want the universe, not the whole wide world. Just this and nothing more: *Make me feel something, anything, in cold water, on a bed of ice, on a night so dark it's impossible to tell the difference between the earth and the sky. Let it happen again and again, time after time. Hurt me so I know I'm still alive.*

II

ARE PEOPLE DRAWN TO EACH OTHER BECAUSE OF THE stories they carry inside? At the library I couldn't help but notice which patrons checked out the same books. They appeared to have nothing in common, but who could tell what a person was truly made of? The unknown, the riddle, the deepest truth. I noticed them all: the ones who'd lost their way, the ones who'd lived their lives in ashes, the ones who had to prove themselves, the ones who, like me, had lost the ability to feel.

I kept going out to the orange grove. It didn't make sense, and it didn't have to. It was as though I had one map inside my head and it led to the man who was waiting for me. Someone who was as alone — maybe even more alone — than I was; someone whose story dovetailed with mine — burned alive, trapped in ice. I thought about Jack Lyons — I might have learned how to be human with him, but what good would that have done? There was so much more to learn from Lazarus. After the first few times we were together, I had gotten up the courage to ask what it had been like to be dead. I'd pleaded to know, but he wouldn't tell me. All the same, I wouldn't let it go. I nagged and begged. Did it hurt, was it heavenly, was there white light or the darkest agony? Lazarus refused to say. He had a beautiful smile, one that made me want him even more. Want, I had discovered, was a country of its own. Everything else drops off the map: oceans, continents, friends, family, the *before,* the *after* — all of it gone.

Throughout the summer the only thing I could think about was the road to Lazarus's. I'd dream about it: the stop signs, the white line, the turnoff, the front porch, the door. My brother phoned and left a few messages, but I didn't bother calling back.

"Are you alive?" Ned's familiar voice asked one day when I played my phone-message tape.

Actually, yes, I wanted to tell him. Amazingly, incredibly enough, I seemed to be. But he wouldn't understand. How could I explain that on rainy nights Lazarus and I sat out on his porch in the dark, drawn there by whatever was inside us, some external weather trapped and mirrored inside our blood and bones. I felt addicted, to the danger, the rush of being alive, taking chances. We had sex outside, in the dark, with the rain coming down. We went down to the pond, turned away from each other, took off our clothes. We didn't have to see each other to know what we wanted. It was a story that no one else knew.

Now when I went to the survivor group I felt nothing, no kinship. I wanted to run away from their sorrowful tales of lives gone wrong. I came late, left early, avoided the girl with the mismatched socks when I saw her on the street. We were nearing hurricane season, a time when lightning-strike survivors feel more stress than usual. Anything can happen at any time. In group, we were told safety tips. Stay away from windows; have a hurricane cellar. And there I was on the porch on nights when the wind nearly carried us away. I wasn't thinking of safety at all.

"Where've you been?" Renny asked me at the snack table after one survivor meeting. There were oatmeal cookies and cream cheese brownies and some gray thing I supposed was red velvet cake, allegedly a specialty around here.

Lately, I'd been more selfish than ever. I had a secret dark world and it suited me. In my greed, I had forgotten about Renny. I was that sort of friend, I suppose, the bad sort, and I was embarrassed by my own self-involvement. Renny looked nervous and underfed. Not that he was my responsibility.

"Here and there," I said.

"You're fucking him?" Renny said. Just like that. As though he could read my mind. Did it show? Surely, I had no expression on my face. I never did.

"Good Lord, you are suspicious." I took a cookie, though I hated oatmeal. "And nasty."

Renny wasn't so easily fooled. "You mean smart."

"I actually did mean that."

We both laughed.

"You, on the other hand," he said. "Very stupid."

"And your romantic life is something to boast about?"

Iris McGinnis. The girl who didn't know he was alive.

"Good one," Renny said. "You got me."

The basis for my friendship with Renny was our shared

chapter on pain. It was an inclusive chapter, the guiding principle of all that was to follow: Careful what you feel. Better yet, feel nothing at all. With his gloves, Renny could not feel enough and had difficulty picking up a straw or a stone. Barehanded, there was too much sensation, dizzying, all-encompassing. Because I'd seen him less once I began to go out to the orchard, I didn't understand how bad his pain had become until that night at group. He looked more anxious than usual; the summer semester was ending and Renny had very little faith in himself.

I was at the library the next day when Renny called on me. I had to show up for work occasionally, but I took my time, slowly, lazily replacing books on their proper shelves, in the dream state I entered whenever I thought about Lazarus. I was the Ice Queen who wanted to be burned alive. I wanted to take the path full of stones that led through the forest of ashes. At the end of that path I would find what every fairy-tale creature yearned for. Not pearls, not kingdoms, not gold. I was looking for something better than that. Real treasure. Real truth.

"You've got to help me," Renny pleaded.

"Is this about Iris again?" Iris McGinnis, nymph of sorrow, so far away she might as well have been living on the moon. Renny loved to talk about her. I usually just tuned him out and let him drone on, but my patience was wearing thin.

"Not Iris. Not this time."

He was failing his architecture course; his end-of-the-summer term project was due and he couldn't work on it himself because of the pain in his hands. He was taking

Demerol, along with Tegretol for the tremors. I could feel guilt rise up inside me like a living being. I wanted to tell him no. After work I planned to get in my car and drive to the secret country where oranges were white. I wanted to walk into the cold pond where Lazarus and I went swimming on clear nights, after all the workers had left, after the trucks had been loaded up and driven away, after it was dark. The mud between my toes under a black and starless sky. I'd been thinking about it all day as I shelved books. I wanted to be dragged under, forget there was anything else in the universe.

But how could I deny Renny, my friend, Renny the sorrowful? How could I tell him what I really wanted? *Go away, go away. I'm in a different country now, one where no one can find me, one where there's no difference between fire and water.*

I should have advised him to pick a new major. But no. Always the volunteer, I offered to do the work if he would instruct me. Renny came over that night. I could tell he was desperate. We were that much alike. His tremor was worse. His hair was long, knotted. He hadn't bathed. All the signs of despair. It was my clicking that kicked in when I felt that way. Sometimes I couldn't hear the TV over the sounds in my own head.

"You're sure you're up for this?" I asked.

Had he been drinking, smoking weed? His eyes were red. And then I thought, *Oh, no.* He'd been crying.

Renny gazed at his gloves; from his expression he might have been looking down at cloven hooves or a lion's paws. "Maybe it's time for me to give up architecture."

Like drawn to like, story to story. I should have said, *Yes, give it up; study literature or art history* — any discipline he might have a chance at rather than a field of study that would surely lead to failure. But that wasn't the way it was going to happen. Jump down the well, sleep for a hundred years, tie yourself to a tree at the base of the mountain, the one where snow falls every day and the ice is ten feet thick.

"Don't be silly." Here I went, pushing him down the well. "Architects don't actually do the building. They inspire and create. Carpenters do all the work."

"I should give it all up. Architecture and Iris. Ridiculous dreams."

"Give up and it will never happen."

I sounded like a character out of an Andersen story, on the side of reason and goodness. I was his cheerleader, his friend, his familiar, his liar. Step up and make the leap. Don't bother with a helmet or a life preserver. You can do it if you really try! Walk on glass, pull the sliver of ice from your heart, face up to it. Overcome.

I sounded so false to myself, but Renny grinned, won over. I suppose people needed stories like Andersen's sometimes. The should-be story, the could-be tale. Renny ran a gloved hand through his messy hair. "I don't have a chance," he said, but I could hear it in his voice — he was being co-erced into believing.

"Let's do it." I always got in too deep. I didn't even want to be here, now I was committing to a major project. "First the temple, then Iris. Inspire me. Boss me around. Treat me like a carpenter."

Renny had brought over glue, sticks, balsa wood, bamboo,

Plexiglas, paper. He unfurled the blueprints on the counter-
top. Truthfully, now that it was before me, the task terrified
me. I had never built anything. Destruction was my game.
Renny took note of my expression.

"Fuck it all," he said. "Maybe I'm supposed to fail."

I cleared off my kitchen table and set out a large sheet of
clear plastic Renny had brought along for the base of the
project. We were to construct a Doric temple, if we could
ever get the cat out of the room, something we finally man-
aged by setting an opened can of tuna on the porch. I was
directed to begin with thin sticks of bamboo. Renny in-
structed me, but the anxiety of ruining the project made me
sweat. I never did anything right, why had I assumed I
could help him?

"Terrific," Renny kept telling me whenever I was able to
connect the bamboo with thin wire. "Excellent."

All the same, it looked like a temple of bones when I'd
finished what was supposed to be the framework. "Are you
sure this is right?" I peered at the blueprints. Sixty percent of
Renny's grade would be based on this project.

"It's just the skeleton," he assured me. "We'll do the rest
next time."

We ordered a pizza delivered, then locked the kitchen to
keep Giselle from knocking over the temple. I had the fan
on, but with it or without it, the clicking inside my head had
grown quieter.

"When it's done, I'm giving the temple to Iris," Renny
told me. "I planned it out at the beginning of the summer."

"Really," I said. I had the shivers; this could lead some-
place dark. Did Iris even know he existed?

Renny opened his wallet and shook out a small gold charm imprinted with the shape of Iris's namesake. It was sad and beautiful and tiny in his huge gloved hand.

"I had this made up by the jeweler at the Smithfield Mall. We'll hang it over the doorway. I'll bet no one ever made something like this for her."

"Renny." Obsession or love, or both? He could read my pity and my doubt.

"You think I'm an idiot. You think I have no chance at all."

"I'm not sure I think anyone has a chance," I admitted.

When the pizza was delivered, Renny paid, treating me to dinner as a thank-you for all my handiwork. When he handed over the cash, the delivery guy stared at Renny's gloves — wary, I suppose, that Renny had some communicable disease.

"He's an idiot," I said of the deliveryman when he had gone. "Pay no attention."

Renny put the gold charm back into his wallet; it took him a long time to do so, he was clumsy and careful both. Usually, I didn't notice Renny's gloves any more than I noticed Giselle's paws. I noticed now. I thought of Iris McGinnis, without a care, leading the life of a college student, not thinking of dark love, gold tokens, Doric temples.

I could feel a change in the air pressure; I leaned out the door and called for the cat. Giselle raced inside and trotted to a corner. She ignored our dinner on the coffee table. Not typical. She had caught something again. Little feet. Gray shadow.

"Is that thing alive?" Renny asked.

"She kills whatever she can get her fangs into." I apologized for Giselle. "It's her nature."

Renny went to the corner and battled the cat for this second mole. She sank her teeth into his glove. "God, she's vicious. Drop it!" he commanded.

The cat wasn't about to take orders, so Renny grabbed her by the neck and gave her a little shake. I suppose Giselle was mortified — I treated her like an equal — she growled and let go, then stalked away, hissing. "Murderess," I called after her. My pet, my dear. I was getting attached to her. I worried when she wouldn't come in at night; I waited anxiously in the yard until she sauntered up in her own good time. She'd stare me down. Then rub herself against my legs. I'd begun to buy cream for her. Bad sign. No attachments, that was my motto. None at all.

"He's got teeth marks in him." Renny had picked up the mole.

"Is he dead?"

Our pizza was getting cold, but I came to examine the mole. It wasn't moving.

"I've got another one out on the porch."

"Seriously? Another mole?"

I brought Renny out to where I'd left the shoebox. I lifted the cover. "This one's definitely dead."

"Are you collecting them?"

We laughed, but it wasn't funny. There in the shoebox was the little fallen-leaf mole, curled up, not much more than skin and bones. Could it be that I'd even become attached to this poor little thing? It smelled like dust and earth, a sad, bitter scent.

"Well, this one's alive," Renny said of today's mole. He put it in his jacket pocket. "I'll bet that one was alive, too. Just playing dead. It's difficult to tell, you know."

I was still the death-wish girl. Touch you once and you turn to ice. Twice and you might disappear.

"Did you check to make sure before you threw him away?" Renny asked.

After all I'd done for him tonight Renny seemed to be accusing me of murder, or, if not that, thoughtlessness. Same difference. I had glue on my hands and my numb fingertips were raw from attaching those damned bamboo sticks. It was never going to work, not my life or his. I was annoyed and I couldn't hide it.

"Maybe we'd better call it quits on the project," I said. "If I do everything wrong, how am I going to construct a temple?"

"So, you're done with me now? Is that it? Why not? Everyone else wants to get rid of me."

He was so sensitive a single drop of poison could affect him, a word, a look, one sliver of ice. He had his head down. He was checking on the mole. I saw what I didn't want to see: Renny was brokenhearted. Like and like. I knew how he felt.

"I don't mean it that way, Renny." I came up beside him, close. My only friend. I could see that the mole was breathing softly. Now I noticed that one of its ears had been torn in half.

I told Renny about Lazarus, not everything, of course, not the way I felt inside, just how I arose from bed at odd hours, compelled to drive out there; I revealed the corners of what was happening. Yet I said too much. Be careful whom you

tell your story to. As we sat on my porch, both of us feeling
the change in the weather, knees touching knees, I made the
mistake of mentioning that Lazarus and I were always to-
gether in the dark. I suppose it was something that nagged
at me. As soon as I'd said it I knew that I should have kept
my mouth shut.

"And that doesn't worry you? You're suspicious about
everything else, but not that? Clearly, there's something this
Lazarus doesn't want you to see. Hell, I wish I could do the
same with Iris. But even in the dark, I wouldn't be able to
trick her. What's wrong with me would be even more obvi-
ous. The dark makes it worse for me."

Renny decided he would show me this final effect of his
strike. The one he kept from everyone. I had the feeling this
might be the deep secret, the riddle of who he was. I wasn't
certain I wanted to know. But there was no stopping him.

The whole thing was much too personal. I wanted out. I
wanted solitude. I wanted to tell him not to show me. I
wanted to say I only appeared to be someone who was inter-
ested and concerned. But I just sat there next to him. Frozen.

Renny took off his gloves. I could hear him doing it; he
grunted with the pain, the rub of the leather against his ru-
ined skin. And then I saw. Amazing. Bits of yellow and
green glowed on his skin. It was so strange, and in some way
quite beautiful. You could see it only in the dark, the gold in
his skin had been woven into him, as though he were a tap-
estry. The gold went beyond the area where his watch and
ring had branded him, as though the metal had been splat-
tered over his hands. But I understood why he feared love as
much as he wanted it: he didn't look quite human.

"They did a biopsy to see if it could be extracted, but the gold is mixed in with the fat and tissue under the skin. I'll never get rid of it."

I gently took his hands in mine. I felt like crying. I wondered if damaged people ever got over what had damaged them.

"So you're made out of gold. It's better than plain flesh."

"Yeah, right. I'm a freak." Renny went to put the porch light on. He kept his back to me and pulled his gloves on. "And so is he, I'll bet. Your friend Lazarus."

Like understands like. I believed that. Renny turned back to me.

"He's hiding something," my friend said.

I never should have told him. Never talked to him. Never gotten involved. "Well, then, I hope it's something as beautiful as your hands."

Renny looked at me as though I were a total fool. "Don't you get it? You don't hide what you think is beautiful. You hide what's broken. You hide when you're a monster."

We dropped the subject, but it was too late. Certain ideas, once they're planted, grow in spite of you. I had begun to think about broken things.

"What do you think moles eat?" Renny asked when I drove him back to the university.

Of course he was going to keep the mole, turn this blind, wounded creature into a pet. What then? Would the mole speak to him? Would he grant Renny three wishes? *Take the gold from my skin, the ring from my fingers, the watch from my wrist?*

"Grubs?" I guessed. "My brother would know, but he's too busy to talk to me."

"Grub stew." Renny grinned. "Grub cakes."

"They probably sell mole food in the pet store. Or try Acres' Hardware. They seem to have everything."

I was thinking of how Ned used to leave out food for the bats that nested in our roof. He'd set a mixture of suet and honey and fruit in the rain gutters. I'd hide my head under my pillow, but he'd watch from the window.

They can find it without seeing where they're going, my brother told me. *That's how defined their senses are. They fly blind through the dark.*

At night the quad at Orlon University was quiet. I felt as though I were delivering Renny to the wrong place, though. It was his brokenness. The campus was so groomed, so perfect, and he was falling apart. A true friend would have been able to weave gloves out of reeds and moleskin for Renny; when he wore gloves such as those for three days in a row, he'd be cured. The first girl who passed by him in the cafeteria would fall in love with him, and it would be Iris. Iris McGinnis would truly look at him, she'd look inside him, and when she saw the way he loved her, she'd be so moved she'd begin to weep.

Renny reached into his pocket for the mole. He was right about me. I probably would have assumed it was beyond help and tossed it into the shoebox with its predecessor to become skin and bones, another curled-up leaf. I wouldn't have even checked for a heartbeat.

"Still alive," Renny said.

"Can't ask for more than that. Can we?"

"Forget what I said about Lazarus. Maybe I was jealous that you've found someone."

As if I could forget. If there was a negative point, I clung to it. A life raft of doubt and fear.

"Sure. Don't worry about it." I was trying for cheerful ease. "And it's not like we're running off to the chapel anytime soon. It's not love, Renny. It's nothing like that."

"I'm happy for you. Whatever it is. I mean it."

He was. He could be brokenhearted and still be happy for someone else.

"I'm going to forget about Iris. It was a stupid idea to give her the temple. Or to ever think she would want me. What would she want with a monster?"

"You're not a monster."

I could feel something hot behind my eyes. It was compassion. Something I didn't want to feel.

"Look, Renny, even if it's not Iris, someone will think you're perfect the way you are." He looked at me and I could tell, no matter what he might say, he still had hope. He wanted to believe. "Trust me," I said.

"Maybe you're right," he said.

"You know it."

I had almost convinced myself. Renny got out of the car and walked backward so he could wave to me.

"Monsters of the world, unite." He raised his gloved fist in the air.

"Go study, or something," I called to him.

He walked into his dorm. He was gone, but not completely. For there it was, still with me: Renny's idea, replay-

ing itself, getting bigger. What if Lazarus was hiding some-
thing? What if he was indeed a monster? The man I thought
I knew could easily be a figment of my imagination, a bear, a
snake, a spiny toad. The more I thought about it, the more I
wondered. Was it possible to know anyone, truly? Could
knowledge hurt, pierce your heart, break your bones?

Instead of going home, I drove to the library. To hell with
human beings. I'd always felt safer with stories than with
flesh and blood. I let myself in the back entranceway with
my key, then locked the door behind me. It was hot and
damp in the library; no wonder the pages of the older edi-
tions were turning brown. I switched on the desk lamp. A
small circle of yellow light. Frances left the desk tidy and
well organized, so I was careful not to displace anything.
There was a peculiar heaviness in the room; during the day
we kept the old air conditioner on, now the dust had settled.
I coughed and the sound echoed.

Frances had photographs of nieces and nephews dis-
played, of a black dog called Harry, of the canals of Venice,
where she'd vacationed last year. Beside my desk, nothing.
Nothing obvious, at least. Just the invisible picture I always
brought with me, the one of myself, the girl who stomped
her feet on the porch, breath billowing out like smoke, little
beast, long dark hair falling down her back, the stars in the
black sky forever set in place, the ice forever shining, brighter
than the stars.

I could hear beetles hitting against the screens in the win-
dows. I heard a sigh, as though the books were breathing. I
felt that this was where I belonged. This was where I lived.
Everything else that had happened or would happen was a

dream of some sort. Then I heard a thud. I took in my breath. A real live noise. That woke me up. Maybe I wanted to be alive, after all. Maybe I wanted to be in the world. I was afraid that a thief was trying to enter the library. Everything was free here; there was nothing to steal. Whoever was crazy enough to break in might also be crazy enough to do more.

I shrank back into the dark. There was a clanging then, and I breathed easier. Not a break-in, a return. I realized that someone had slipped a book through the night drop. Nothing more. I pinched myself for being an idiot and went to the door. Nothing to be afraid of. I could see someone dressed in white walking down the path. She was barefoot on the concrete. Her hair was pale and she was in a hurry. There was a car parked in the street, left running. The night was dark, black as beetles. I couldn't make out any features until the car door opened and there was a flash of light. The woman was my sister-in-law.

I stood watching until the car disappeared. My heart was pounding. Too fast. Too hard. I had spent my life feeling as though I were an accomplice to a crime. It was nothing new to me. Death-wisher, betrayer, liar, secret-keeper. I was death's assistant, with no great skill of my own. A lackey, a fool, the helpmate whose every move had resulted in tragedy. One step, one wish, one mistake, one icy night. And now I had seen my sister-in-law, Nina, rushing to her car, driving off into the dark. I realized the white thing she was wearing was her nightgown.

The book she'd left was in the night-drop bin; when I picked it up it was still warm from her touch. I took the

book with me, out the back door, where my car was parked
in the shadows. I drove back through the campus, and it was
probably no accident that I wound up on my brother's street.
Maybe I wanted to be reassured that it hadn't been Nina at
the library, only someone who looked like her. I could see
into some of the houses, filled with yellow light, with life.
My brother's house, however, was dark. Everyone asleep.
Everyone safe inside. The car I'd seen at the library was
parked in the driveway. Maybe she hadn't driven it tonight;
all the same, I wasn't sure I wanted to know. I didn't dare get
out and touch the hood of the car to see if it was still warm.

There was a streetlight above me; when I flipped over the
book that had been returned I saw the title: *A Hundred Ways
to Die.* It was the instruction manual for suicide I'd often re-
ferred to in New Jersey when Jack Lyons phoned me for in-
formation. I felt something close up in my throat. I'd
thought that like always recognized like, but it seemed I'd
been completely mistaken about Nina.

I watched the beetles fly through the dark above their
lawn. I wondered if Nina had reached home and had
crawled into bed beside my brother, if he hadn't even no-
ticed she'd been gone, noticed her pale feet were cold. Now I
remembered that the day before my mother died, my
brother had spent all day making her a present. It was a
book made of construction paper, bound with shoelaces.
When I'd asked him what it was, he'd said it was the story of
his life. *That's stupid,* I'd said. I didn't look at his face to see if
I'd hurt him. *Who cares about that?* I was jealous. I knew a
book could make something real. In this case, it was his love
right there on that paper, tied with laces, given over freely to

our mother. That's why I'd been so mean to Ned. I had nothing. I hadn't even thought to give her a present. I hadn't thought at all.

The house we'd lived in in New Jersey could have easily fit into the living room of the house where my brother lived now. It was a beautiful structure, even in the dark. Before tonight I had imagined that Ned and Nina slept well at night, logical sleep, dreamless and sweet. Now I looked through the shadows to see there was a woman on the lawn. My brother's wife. In her nightgown she was almost invisible. But she was there. It was Nina. She didn't move at all. I tried to get away quickly, before she could see me. I began to drive away, headlights switched off. Maybe this had never happened, maybe I'd been all wrong, but when I turned to look out the rear window I saw that she had spied me, not that she seemed to care. She looked right through me, as if this world no longer concerned her, as if everything that mattered could no longer be seen with the naked eye.

True

I

PEOPLE HIDE THEIR TRUEST NATURES. I UN-
derstood that; I even applauded it. What sort of
world would it be if people bled all over the
sidewalks, if they wept under trees, smacked
whomever they despised, kissed strangers, re-
vealed themselves? Keep a cloak, that was fine,
the thing to do; present a disguise, the outside
you, the one you want people to believe. My
sister-in-law was a perfect example: the sunny,
near-perfect mathematician who drove through

the quiet streets in her nightgown when most good people were in bed, who studied the hundred ways to die. I had already decided I wouldn't mention the fact that I'd seen her at the book deposit. A liar like all the rest, ready to pretend I didn't know about the crack in the reality of her life, the dark hour, the library door, the book of sorrow in her hands.

Absinthe, that's how it began — ingested, of course. Anemia caused by refusing all food, anonymity, arsenic, asphyxiation, barbiturates (crumbled into puddings or applesauce to make for speedy digestion), bee stings (see wasps, see nests, see allergies), belladonna, black hellebore (brewed into a tea), cars (accident, asphyxiation), crucial arteries (knives, razors, ballpoint pens), death by drowning, falls from open windows (eighth floor or above), fire, gas ovens, gunshot wounds, hanging, heroin, death by ice, ivy (pulverized and made into soup or tea), jimsonweed, OxyContin, pennyroyal, plastic bag over the head (see double death, see ensuring overdose), poison hemlock, the root of pokeweed, ponds and lakes, death by provoked police incident (see car chase, public drunkenness, public nuisance), public restrooms, renting motel rooms, sedatives, standing in the wrong place at the wrong time, stimulants, death by wishes.

I had seen Nina in passing since that night at the library, once at the market, another time in the cafeteria while Renny and I ate lunch; both times she'd waved cheerfully to me. I simply waved back, then went about my business as though I hadn't skimmed through *A Hundred Ways to Die* before returning it to the shelf, as though my sister-in-law hadn't been standing on the library steps in her nightgown. Self-help, that's the section where it belonged.

The truth was, I didn't want to interfere. Why should it be up to me to touch anyone's life, guide someone right rather than left, off the road instead of on? Get involved and you made mistakes. Inevitable. Who knows where your advice, interest, love, might lead? Start and it might be impossible to stop. That was what was happening with Lazarus. I had taken the one bead of doubt Renny had tossed out and strung a necklace, red pearls, invisible to my eye, but tight around my throat, pulling at me.

Who was he really? That was the question. What did it mean to have a lover who would embrace you only in the dark? Who wanted to conceal not only his deepest self but everything on the surface? Nothing good, that was certain; nothing you could trust. Something unexpected that was sure to bite you and bring you down. How easy it was to be undone by some things. By these things. Red pearls. Truth. What you don't want to know, need to know, have to keep in the palm of your hand. Grab it, the stinging nettle, the wasp, the shard of glass. Do it. Then live with the consequences.

Whenever I asked Lazarus what it had been like to be dead, he would laugh. *I told you, we're not talking about that.* He had his rules: *this,* but not *that.* In the dark, all night long, but never in the light. But I wouldn't let it go. When did I ever? I whispered and prodded like a nagging wife, a child who wouldn't give up. Stomp your feet, little girl. Hack off your hair for spite. Get what you want. Don't give up. Needle, beg, cry.

Were there welcoming family members? A black hole? Did time stretch out into infinity, or was it a single slam, poof, *over,*

like a magician passing a kerchief over a rabbit, and then gone,
gone, gone?

He laughed at me. It was a hundred degrees at the time
and we were in the kitchen, shades drawn. Lazarus was
wearing a long-sleeved white shirt. Now I noticed: every
button was buttoned.

"Why don't you think about right here, right now?"

Lazarus put his arms around me, pulled me close into his
burning chest, had his mouth to my ear. His voice itself was
hot, melting me. I felt him against me, thigh to thigh, and at
that moment I believed I knew him. In a way. Hot, night,
fuck, kiss, skin, muscles, heat. The way his arms felt in the
dark. Each rib. Ladder, cage, his, mine. The size and heat of
him inside me. The words he said that weren't words at all.
The way he wanted me. Wasn't that enough? Couldn't that
be love? The very science of it was all there: heart racing,
the mind willing to believe almost anything; she longs for
the dark, wants him when she's not with him, gets in the car
at all hours, drives down dark roads. More symptoms? An
elevated pulse rate, the center of the self moves lower, into
the abdomen, sex, thighs, the unthinking, the undoing, the
you not alone, the you disappeared, the no difference be-
tween inside and outside. All the signs. Proof enough of an
attachment.

And yet there it was. The power of a single idea in my
head. What was hidden, what was not. It was a tape inside
me, one I couldn't rewind. It was a bird's voice, a mole's
whisper: *Find out.*

Isn't that the center of every story? The search for the
truth. The need to know. Tear off the sealskin, the donkey-

skin, the feathers, the shackles. In moonlight, starlight, lan-
ternlight, bluelight. Wasn't that what everyone wanted: to
see and hear. Take the veil from my eyes. The stones from
within my ears. Turn me around twice. Tell me. No matter
the consequence. No matter the price. At least until it has to
be paid. At least until the price blinds you, deafens you,
burns you alive.

When I next went to see Lazarus, I sneaked a look at the
bookshelves in the living room while he was working in the
study. Paying bills. Having the iced tea I'd made him. Busy.
Trusting me. Of all people. The bookshelves were dusty.
The whole room was. Bluelight, lanternlight. None of the
books had been touched for some time. As a librarian I
could gauge such things, what was in use, what wasted
away. The layer of dust, the way the book sat on the shelf,
unwanted and unused. I went from one bookcase to another.
More travel. Guidebooks to France. Museums in New York.
Peruvian villages. An entire shelf of Italy. All of it alphabet-
ized, so orderly, so dusty. A museum of books.

Lazarus came into the room and caught me on my hands
and knees.

"Getting ready for me?" he said.

He laughed. So did I.

I should have been embarrassed; there was so much about
sex between us. I wondered how it would be if we didn't
need ice, water, all that cold. If given half the chance, we
would never stop; maybe we'd grind each other into ashes,
into dust, burning hot, bloodred.

"I'm looking at the books." I turned away. I always did
that when I didn't trust something or someone.

"You don't see enough of them at the library? Is that it?"

He was closer, his hands on the waistband of my jeans, fingers dipping close enough to burn my skin.

"If you're going to be reading to me, make it a bedtime story." He grinned, sly. I liked that grin. I liked what he meant. I suppose I flushed. My face was probably red. Rose. Blush. Not embarrassment. Ardor. All of the wanting I had, that much I couldn't hide. We spent most of our time in the bathtub; we had sex the way fish must, in waves, in the cold, skins shivering into scales. When we were in the bed, we were on top of a blanket of crushed ice. My fingers turned blue; I didn't care. They were numb anyway, unless I was touching him.

I waved a book in front of him. It smelled like green fields, red wine, sunlight. The subtle scent of printer's ink. "You're interested in Italy?"

"I'm interested in you."

He probably thought that was the answer I wanted.

It could have been. It might have been. Except it wasn't.

"Seriously. You've got so many travel books. You're not about to disappear on me, are you? Go off to Rome or Florence? You could find yourself another woman, someone pretty."

He took the book out of my hand. Could anyone be looking at me that way?

"You're the one I want."

I believed him. I should have stopped. But it had already begun, the plan I had, the need I had, the direction we were stumbling into, the middle of our story, the most dangerous part, when anything at all can happen.

Lazarus blew the dust off the book and returned it to the shelf. The books were in order, city by city, country by country. He stuck the book into the South American section. He didn't care about order. All at once I had the sense that he'd never seen this book before. This or any other on the shelf.

"Maybe we should go somewhere." I wanted a reaction. The way children poke at dead things with sticks. Alive or not? Vicious or tame? "I'm serious. Someplace we've never been before."

He looked at me. Ten years younger. The sort of man who should have never bothered with me. Beautiful. Didn't he know that? Hadn't he ever looked in a mirror? Or was it me he couldn't see? Was it situational blindness — I couldn't see red; he couldn't see ugliness or deceit.

But he felt something was wrong. It was in the air, like dust motes or gnats. There was a ridge between his eyes. As though he was trying to figure out why I'd be talking about going away when everything we wanted should have been right here.

"Hey, come into the kitchen," he said. "I fixed you lunch."

Just like that. Not interested. Next subject. The *here and now*. Lunch on the table. Like normal folks.

I followed him down the hall. I had a blank feeling, as if somebody had taken what little there was inside me and blown it away. Now I was sure — he'd never read the books on his shelf.

For lunch he'd fixed me hot tomato soup. He liked it cold himself, with ice mixed in. He poured himself a glass of fresh orange juice.

"Vitamin D," he said.

He needed to think about such things. His complexion was pale; he was never in the sun. I thought he might be fading in front of my eyes. I thought about the field-worker who had half believed he was working for a monster. I sat at the table. We didn't have much to say. Outside the oncoming dusk was undulating, moving between the clouds in waves of blue light. I felt heartbroken and I hadn't even known I had a heart to break.

That's the danger when you come to the middle of the story. You may find out more than you ever wanted to know.

We stayed in the kitchen and watched the light fading in the orchard. All that blue, all that light. If I stayed, I would rinse the dishes and he would rest his hands on the ice in the freezer, then come up behind me and touch me until I was burning. I'd let the tap water run. I'd put my cold, wet arms around him. But that's not what happened that day. We were moving into the after; the *then* and the *now* and the *soon will be* were becoming separate realms.

This had been happiness and we didn't know it. We walked right past. Had no idea. Step after step.

I felt a stinging somewhere, a sharpness. We were waking from the dream of the kitchen, the afternoon, the way we wanted each other. When it grew dark we usually went into the bedroom, the bath. We were happy for the night. Now I was tired. It had been a long day. And we still weren't done. I told him I didn't feel well. I needed my sleep. I wasn't ready to find out anything, I suppose. Not yet. I knew the truth would turn things around.

"Sorry," I said when he walked me out to the porch.

"Sorry for what?"

For nothing. For everything. For all I was about to do. "For being tired."

He grabbed me and I kissed him until my mouth was burning. No ice. Not this time. He let me go, looked at me.

"I don't want to hurt you," Lazarus said.

That's what they all said, and then they went ahead and did anyway. When I drove home, I felt bereft.

I'd lost something; I felt it as surely as I had when I lost the color red, a color I'd never even liked, one I avoided. Now every shade was faded without it, drained, not just scarlet and crimson and vermilion but even rust seemed gray; coppers and bronzes were flat without their red tones. Without red, the dawn was milk, rubies were worthless.

I didn't trust him. That was the loss. Dropped like a stone into a pool. Not a word he said, not a book he'd read, not a fuck or a kiss or a look. Not a bowl of soup. Nothing.

I went home and there was my cat, tail waving back and forth, crouched by the hedge. Every flower was as white as chalk. She ignored me when I walked up the path, but came running when I opened the door to the screen porch. Foul-weather friend. She was due to be fed. She knew what she wanted; I was the one who couldn't tell if she was purring or if her stomach was merely rumbling as she rubbed against my legs.

My porch. My key. My home. My nothing.

There was the shoebox, atop the carton filled with old newspapers, grocery bags, odds and ends. I couldn't bring myself to bury the mole, and I couldn't toss it out with the trash. I thought about Renny. We had been working on the Doric temple, and it was nearly done. He had to finish, and he'd been calling me, trying to set up a time when we could get together. But I was busy, too preoccupied to hear about his classes or how the mole he'd saved was thriving, getting fat on cream and grubs. I did agree to work with him on the coming Sunday, but he'd have to wait till then. I had my own problems to think about.

I peeked inside the box where the dead mole was kept. Some ants had gotten into the mess. There was a smell of damp skin, earth, rot. Nothing pretty. Nothing to keep. Looking at the box, I realized I couldn't let go; not even of this. I'd been that way all my life, holding on tight. I couldn't let go of anything.

Except for the things that mattered most.

I HAD AN APPOINTMENT WITH MY CARDIOLOGIST SOON after. Craven. The man who insisted I had a heart. I'd stupidly complained of pain in my chest the last time I'd been to see him, and now he fitted me with a heart monitor that I was to wear for twenty-four hours.

"You have arrhythmia — and even though that's not unusual for people who've experienced a strike, we want to be careful."

"Is there some congenital defect that hadn't been detected before?" I was thinking of that dreadful Andersen character whose heart is pierced by a shard of ice.

"You're as normal as possible, given the circumstances," Craven said. "We just like to keep watch. In case."

I'd been calling in sick to the library in order to spend more time at the orchard with Lazarus. I'd pretty much used every excuse. Nausea, ears ringing, pain in my arm, my side, my everything. My ailments were half true at least, so my guilt didn't sting as it might have, should have. Obsession did that, I presumed. The wanting of someone, something. The chances a person was suddenly willing to take, the lies so easy to tell. Frances York had never once questioned me or complained. Her generosity should have made it more difficult for me to be selfish, but it didn't. After the doctor, I headed over to work. Once I'd parked and went in, I found I was looking forward to returning. I'd missed it, in fact. All those untrustworthy words were unspoken here, safely printed and bound up tight.

"Are you feeling better?" Frances asked when I arrived straight from my doctor's appointment. It was late, hours past the time I should have shown up had I been working regularly. The weather was muggy and not even the old air-conditioning system could do much about that.

"I'm okay."

Oh, sure. Only sex sick, love sick, lie sick.

Frances studied me. She might be losing her vision, but she was sharp. "Really?"

I pulled up my shirt and showed Frances the contraption strapped across my chest.

"And they said it was all right to come to work?"

Well, here was my chance, so I took it. "Probably not. I have an arrhythmia. They can track my heartbeat this way. But I feel like a horse in a harness. Or a mule."

"You should definitely go home and rest," Frances said.

I thought about Falada, that loyal horse who couldn't help but speak the truth to the Goose Girl, even when his head had been cut off. I suppose I had a moment of remorse, a flash of honesty. It came over me as I stood behind the card catalog.

"I want to be the way I used to be."

It was a stupid thing to say aloud. I didn't even know what it meant. The me I used to be in what place and time? Yesterday? The day before my mother drove away from us? The minute before Renny suggested that Lazarus was hiding his truest self from me?

Frances was concerned. "Any recuperation takes time. Don't rush yourself."

She was making matters worse, being so thoughtful. No wonder I stayed away from kindness; in some ways it was worse than ill treatment. You could fight against cruelty, tooth and claw, but sympathy engulfed you, took you over, made you aware of all you'd done wrong. I realized I knew absolutely nothing about Frances, except the information I'd garnered from the photographs on her desk. Perhaps she also thought she knew me. I suppose she saw my empty cubicle and made her own assumptions. Poor thing, no photos whatsoever, no personal items, no personal life. And now that harness to chart her fluttering heart — why, it only adds to the already pitiful facts: the ridiculous pixie cut on a grown woman, the way she kneels down in the stacks, as though she had a penance to pay, and her dreadful pale skin. Poor creature. Poor me.

I kept thinking about those strange books on Lazarus's shelves. I'd been so sure that our stories were the same, and now I wasn't sure of anything. I didn't begin to sneak about until Frances went to get some takeout. She was picking up a salad for me as well. Something complicated, I made certain of that, so it would surely take a while for the coffee shop to prepare it for me. Feta and onions and fancy lettuce and olives. Not the kind with pimentos, the dark purple ones.

"Are you sure they have that, dear?"

Not at all. But I was sure my order would give me the time alone I needed. I was ready to dig; I was looking for blood and bones. I watched Frances drive away, then quickly looked up Lazarus's card. Seth Jones had indeed taken out guidebooks. His interests were deserts, South America, Florence, Rome, and Venice. I held the card in my hand and stared at the titles. A normal enough card, except for a printed mark at the very top. CONTINUED. This wasn't his only card on file.

I returned it to the catalog. As I did I noticed a card made out for Iris McGinnis; this must be Renny's Iris, the girl of his dreams. What could she find here that wouldn't be in the university library? Perhaps she'd only wanted to take her time — we allowed books to be taken out for a month, and the university had a cutoff of two weeks. She'd borrowed the *Odyssey* and the *Iliad*. A classics major? A slow reader? A woman who preferred mythological creatures?

Maybe I should have jotted down Iris's phone number for Renny, but I was rushed. Frances would be back soon. It was nearing suppertime. I grabbed a flashlight and went down to the basement, to the storeroom. There were boxes of waterlogged books, from the time when the pipes had burst and Frances had enlisted people in town to help save what they could. In the back of the room, finally, I found the old cards. I opened the first box and sifted through the jumble.

Many of the names referenced residents at the home for the aged. Dozens of yellowing cards, lists of withdrawn books belonging to nearly everyone over the age of sixty-five who'd lived in the town of Orlon. And then, Seth Jones. I held his card up to the light that filtered in through the single rectangular window. More travel books, Africa, Hawaii, copies of *National Geographic*. Once again, impossibly so, CONTINUED.

I went on to the next box, the oldest records of all. Most of these cards belonged to people who had already passed on; *deceased* was marked on many in Frances's neat script, then there was some handwriting I didn't recognize, which I assumed belonged to the librarian before Frances. I looked through it all; at last, I found Seth Jones. The very day he'd taken out his first library book had been marked in blue ink, nearly forty-five years earlier. Surely, this was Lazarus's grandfather. Seth Jones would be seventy years or older now, not a beautiful young man who rarely left his house, someone ten years younger than I, a man who was burning hot with eyes made of ashes, someone hiding something, everything, including who he was.

By the time Frances came back with our food, I'd tidied the boxes, piled them back one on top of another, then washed the dust off my hands. Seth Jones's library card was hidden in my desk drawer. Frances had waited for twenty minutes while Renee Platt ran out to the Quickmart to pick up kalamata olives. Now, after all that effort, I couldn't eat. I told Frances there was something wrong with my stomach. Maybe it was the heart monitor pressing down on me. Maybe it was that I was more confused by Lazarus than ever. Why did I still have the sense he was keeping something from me? Wives, bodies, donkeyskin, rooms that should never be entered, stairs that lead to a storeroom of diamonds and bones.

I thought of the mole blindly puttering around the roots of the hedge until there was a sudden rush of teeth and a sharp twist of its neck. I thought about the way I'd knocked at Lazarus Jones's door. I thought of "Ring of Fire," the song people in Orlon listened to against their better judgment. I was starting to have compassion for people who did stupid things. If Iris McGinnis had walked into the library, I would have gone right up to her, had I been able to recognize her, and slapped her. *Don't you know how miserable you're making someone who loves you?* That's what I'd have said to her. *Who do you think you are?*

"Go home," Frances told me. The library had evening hours, but she clearly felt I'd be of no help. I must have looked dazed; clearly I was overwhelmed. I hoped that I'd taped up the boxes in the storeroom correctly, put each in its proper place. I hoped Frances never found out how untrustworthy I was, or if she did, that it was long after I'd gone.

I drove home and stood in my yard. I didn't want to think, really. The possibilities were too terrible. I thought of all those fairy-tale husbands who hadn't known their true loves in the dark. Fools who'd slept with evil queens or murderous sisters while their real wives were chained to tower walls or thrown to the wild beasts in the woods to be torn apart and forgotten. As a child, I hadn't believed such stories. Impossible to be duped in such a way. The lover would always know his beloved, certainly, certainly, without a doubt. I hadn't understood what a mystery a human being was, how many forms love could take.

The Seth Jones on record had had a library card for nearly twice as long as my Seth Jones had been alive. No wonder he'd been taking out an old man's books. No wonder his house was dust-filled, his bookshelves untouched. Either the original Seth Jones was an old man or Lazarus was pretending to be someone he wasn't.

Now I wanted to know whom I'd been sleeping with.

I'd left Giselle out for the day and now she came to rub herself against my legs. Who would ever think that September could be too hot? I watched the cat poke around in the weeds. I wasn't expecting my brother, but he pulled up and honked the horn. Same car as Nina had been driving the other night. It took all my effort to lift my arm and wave.

"I heard you were at the cardiologist today," Ned said as he came to join me. "Old Craven gave me a call."

"Busybody," I said. "Both of you."

"I'm just making sure all the docs in the study treat you right."

Ned had a tall Styrofoam cup in one hand; he went to fetch some lawn chairs from the porch, which he brought down to the scruffy yard, the worst one on the block. Probably the worst for miles around. "Oouf," Ned said as he set the chairs down. "These weigh a ton. Wearing your harness?"

"Twenty-four hours. Then I'm ripping it off."

My brother had stopped at the student union on his way over and picked up a large iced green tea. I supposed the research project he was at work on was taxing; he looked exhausted. He took a sip of his drink.

"You don't like green tea," I reminded him.

Was I supposed to tell him what I knew? Warn him? Protect him? Tell him all about Lazarus Jones? Reveal my secret life, his secret wife? Should I have said, *Your wife isn't who you think she is. She's wandering around in the night, searching for ways to die. Not just one or two, you understand. That's not enough for her. A hundred different ways. Even more than I know, the expert, the death-wisher.*

"Antioxidants," my brother said. "Nina says we should all drink three cups of green tea a day. Oh, and tofu and miso, she's a big fan of those as well." Ned looked happy, as he had at his party. Just the idea of her. Just the thought. He was brightened somehow. Uplifted. He leaned his head against the lawn chair and gazed at the sky. Maybe the moon was red, maybe it was gray; I had no idea. "Did you know you had bats?" Ned asked.

"Very funny."

My brother appeared older now that he'd begun to lose his hair, but when I looked more closely, he was still the same.

"Seriously. Fruit bats. Over by the hibiscus."

The tall hedge covered with large colorless flowers.

"Is that what that is? Hibiscus?" I leaned my head back, too. A black cloud flitted across the sky. Bats. "Shit. You're right."

"You don't have to worry. You don't have hair anymore. Long hair," he corrected when I glared.

"What about you?" I said. Charming me. "You have less."

Ned ignored the remark. He always did that, left you hanging with your own nastiness. "And you're not wearing red or yellow. That's what they're attracted to."

"Shoo." I clapped my hands. My grandmother always told me that would keep bats away. The noise echoed and they left you alone. But the bats in my yard actually came closer.

"They think you're calling to them," my brother said. "They hear it as a love song. That's why they smack into the engines of planes. They think they're being seduced by some huge horny bat made out of metal and then — *kaboom* — crushed, mashed, and decimated."

Proof of my theory: Love destroyed you.

I couldn't help but think of Nina, that book in her hands, her nightgown, her bare feet, the way she looked right through me.

"If I knew a secret," I asked Ned, "would you want me to tell you?"

"A riddle, right?" He grinned. He liked games. The more mathematical the better.

"No. I really want to know, Ned. Would you?"

My brother thought this over. He was wearing a sport shirt and chinos. I hadn't made it to his and Nina's wedding. My grandmother had already been ailing, and I hadn't wanted to leave her, but now I wished I'd managed to attend.

Ned had thought enough. "Secrets are only knowledge that hasn't yet been uncovered," he told me. "Therefore, they're not in fact secrets, but only unrealized truth."

"Bullshit." I snorted and looked up at the bats.

"Is this about your health?" Ned asked. "Because if that's what it is, maybe I should know."

We looked at each other. We were both extremely cautious people. We'd learned the lessons of our childhood. Ask questions, only not too many. Look before you leap. Buy new tires. Be careful whom you love.

"I'm just wearing the heart monitor for my cardiologist's peace of mind. I'm fine. I skip a beat. Who cares? I get to take this contraption off in the morning."

Ned looked relieved. I suppose he still felt responsible. He didn't need to, but he did.

"Now that I know you're all right," he said, "I just want to look at the sky."

Sitting there with my brother, I realized how little we knew about each other; we were like strangers who'd been forced into the same ditch during some vicious, bloody war, and as soon as it was over, we'd gone our separate ways. For an instant I felt like crying. Whenever our mother went out with her friends, Ned would read to me. I always begged for fairy tales, which he'd claimed to despise. I'd thought he read to me only to keep me from whining, to shut me up so I'd go to sleep. Now I wondered if he'd felt responsible back then, if he'd needed comfort as well. I wondered if he'd also wanted to hear those stories.

"If she came back, would we recognize her?" my brother asked.

A funny question from him. I didn't think he wondered about such things.

"We'd know her anywhere." I sounded convinced. But in fact I wondered about that myself. If our mother wandered out from behind the hedge right now, she'd still be thirty, her long blue scarf wrapped around her, her high-heeled boots, her pale hair.

Why are you sitting in the dark? You aren't reading, are you?
You'll ruin your eyes. You'll never get to sleep that way.

I stretched out my legs in the prickly grass. My lawn was
the sort of disaster no one could fix. "We'd know her," I said.
"I think."

"I suppose we would," my brother agreed.

"So, are you sure you don't want to know any secrets?"
Did I mean whether or not we'd truly know our own
mother, lost so long ago, or who I was deep inside, or what
his wife was reading when all the lights were out?

"Do you?"

"You have secrets?" I was surprised. Ned had always
seemed clear to me in some way, perfectly knowable, logical,
a piece of emotional glass.

"Unknown truths," my brother joked. "At least to you.
Known to me, of course. At least in theory. What I know
and what I don't know, I'm not sure I can be the judge of
that."

"Oh, forget it." I was annoyed, the way I'd been with him
when we were children and he seemed more interested in
bats, ants, stars, blowflies, theorems, than in human beings. I
got up and folded my lawn chair. "Thanks for stopping by.
My cardiologist, the worrywart, told me to get a good night's
sleep. Maybe I should listen to him for once."

"I was thinking about the Dragon today," my brother
said. "I never got the chance to interview him."

"The old man in Jacksonville? The one who died twice?"

I felt guilty about my current secret life with a dead man.
But then, my brother didn't want to know any secrets, so he
wouldn't have wanted to know about Lazarus Jones.

"It would have been fascinating — just as an incident. I've tried to contact him three times for our study. He doesn't have a phone. I guess I should give up, the way we did with that Jones character. Chased Sam Wyman off his property with a gun."

I wanted to get the conversation back around to the Dragon.

"So, go see the Dragon. You're not the one who gives up. You never do. That's me."

"Oh, right," my brother said. "Miss Chickenshit."

"Mr. Bullshit," I said right back. It was the way we used to talk to each other, and it was far more comfortable than being polite. It made me miss my childhood. Of all things. I started up toward the porch. I didn't especially want to discuss men who'd died and come back to life. Not with Ned.

"You'd better run." My brother grinned and pointed to the bats in a cloud up above. "Woo-hoo! They might come after you."

"You are so mean." I started to trot, the lawn chair over my shoulder hitting against my ribs. So, I was still nervous about bats, big deal. My brother got up and closed his lawn chair, then followed me to the porch, where we deposited the chairs into a pile of lawn furniture. The porch was a mess, like the rest of my life. Garbage pails. Tools left behind by the previous tenant. Umbrellas. An old orange crate on its side in which Giselle liked to sleep. My brother spied the shoebox. He would.

"What's this?" He opened the box; there was the little leaf of a mole. Dry and ashy now. Bone and fur. "You tried to save something," Ned said.

I laughed. How mistaken my poor brother was. "Idiot. Can't you see? I killed it."

Ned went into the kitchen and came back with a serving spoon. I traipsed after him to the hedge, where he intended to dig a little grave. There were beetles flying about. There was the scent of oranges, even here, miles away from any of the orchards. The circle of bats was high in the sky. They looked as though they could reach the moon.

My brother's knees creaked when he knelt down on the ground. He was thirteen years older than my mother had been on the night she died. He finished digging the grave in no time. He was efficient. Always had been.

Ned took the mole out of the shoebox and placed it in the earth, then covered the body with several hibiscus leaves. I realized I was crying, something I hadn't done at my own mother's funeral. When I deposited my heart monitor at the cardiologist's office in the morning, my doctor would most likely find a spike at exactly this hour. The hour when my brother and I buried something together while the bats flew overhead. The time when I felt something.

I wished my mother would step out from between the hedges. I wished I could take back everything I'd ever done or said or wished. I would throw myself at her feet and ask her to forgive me. She'd be kind, I knew that. She was that way, and would be still. She'd tell me to stand up, to forgive and forget; she'd tell me she wasn't one to hold a grudge. That her heart was open and always had been; that she was the same as she was, not a day older; that love didn't change like the moon or tides, that it was the single constant in the universe.

But here was the thing — even if I did know her, I wasn't certain she would recognize me. A strange woman in the dark, all grown up, standing in the grass, under the moon, beneath a cloud of bats, crying at a funeral for a leaf, a mole, a lost love, an idea.

"Well, that's done," my brother said.

He clapped the dirt from his hands and the bats came closer. "What'd I tell you. Poor schmucks. They're drawn to sound."

He knew I was crying, but was too polite to mention it. Just as I was too polite to suggest that his wife was someone he didn't really know.

"Well, thanks," I said. "I would have kept it forever."

We laughed at the way I held on to things. I didn't even like to throw out my garbage; I had a month's worth of old newspapers stacked in the hall.

"Let go," my brother told me.

"You first."

Exactly what we used to say when we both wanted the same thing — the last cookie in the box, the last soda in the fridge.

We looked at the moon.

"Is it red?" I wanted to know.

"Any color you see is refracted by the water molecules in the air. It's stone-colored, however it appears, kiddo. It's gray."

Regardless, it was certainly the most beautiful full moon of the year. In New Jersey it would be rising over birch trees, marshes turning brown, papers blowing down the sidewalks.

It was probably the color of a human heart.

"You'd be able to float if you were walking up there," my brother told me.

I thought about that after Ned left to go home. I thought about how he'd called me in from the porch when my mother drove away and how I wouldn't listen. Eventually, of course, I'd had no choice. My feet were freezing; they hurt. At last, I went inside. We were weightless that night. We had both stood at the window together, just for a second, side by side, seeing the very same thing for once in our lives: the long road away from our house, the dark horizon, the future, and everything it could bring.

I I

I BROUGHT A CANDLE WITH ME WHEN I NEXT WENT to the orchard. How many women in how many stories had done this before? Mistrusted a lover, longed for an answer to a question that was not yet fully formed. If a secret was only unrealized knowledge, as my brother had said, what harm could it do? How dangerous could a tiny shred of truth be? It had no thorns, no talons, no teeth nor tail nor sting. Truth, sleeping on the other side of what I knew. Of course, there were a hundred versions of the same story: a woman who has to learn what she already knows, somehow, somewhere inside.

I'd brought matches as well. In my pocket, snug against my hip bone. It was a plan, not an accident. There was no chance involved, no circumstance. It was what I thought I wanted, needed, had to have. I had spent the day waiting for the dark, looking forward to it, the way bats must pine for the last bits of sunlight, green, gold, disappearing from sight. I'd dropped off my heart monitor, then stopped at Acres' Hardware for the candles; I was in the notions aisle when I saw the man who'd been attacked by the bulldog, the patient my physical therapist had told me about. Bitten, torn apart, he was now shelving cans of paint. Even from a distance I could see the marks on his face, tooth and nail.

"I've got the Mandarin Orange," he called to a customer, just as though he were unscarred. And maybe he was. He had managed to be the reverse of most people. In his case he showed the deep, dark riddle; inside, he might be as clear and pure as water.

I went home and waited for the end of the day. My stomach was jumpy. I couldn't eat supper. Renny's project was still in my kitchen. He phoned to check in and I swore we would finish the temple on Sunday; the due date of the project was Monday and without the temple Renny would surely fail. Well, failure was something I knew about. So I promised him, my one and only friend. I assured him we had time. It was Friday now. I had all night. All day tomorrow. Plenty of time to prove my doubts right or wrong.

The sky was even darker than usual, cloudy, no moon in sight. I drove out, my foot heavy on the gas pedal. Florida whirred past me, a dizzying globe. Heat and darkness, beetles hitting against the windshield. I used to walk home from the library in New Jersey feeling lost even though I knew my way. Now I felt found. I passed exits with names I didn't know, towns I'd never been to, but I knew exactly where I was going. Gold and green and black, like a bat drawn to clapping hands in the darkness, against all logic, a love song it was impossible to understand.

He was waiting for me. That surprised me. I couldn't imagine myself mattering to anyone. There was something suspicious in his desire for me. I saw him when I got out of my car, slammed the door shut, smelled oranges. There were moths in the night along with the beetles, and little gnats and mosquitoes. Something bit me and it hurt. I ran to the porch. I wanted to get this over with.

"Hey, you." He rose from the old wooden bench left on the porch for fifty years or more. He was wearing a long-sleeved white shirt, jeans, old boots. I saw him shining there, like a star.

"Hey, you," I said back.

"You're late. I was going to make you some dinner."

Just like normal people. He seemed to want that.

I went to him, reached my arms around him, stood on my toes, started to burn.

He backed away from me, looked into my face. It was just me. I leaned up and kissed him. Once, twice, then I had to stop.

"I missed you," he said.

He kissed me again, hard.

Every fairy tale had a bloody lining. Every one had teeth and claws.

"Baby," I said. I called him that. He was so beautiful, his hands, his ashy eyes, his throat, his everything.

"I could still make soup." He'd opened the screen door for me. I thought I would probably always remember how it sounded. It was the opening into the *after*. It sounded like wind on a quiet night.

"I'm not hungry," I said, the way a starving woman might, so as not to give herself away.

Into the dark hallway, past the coatrack, the jackets, the rain boots, all of it belonging to Seth Jones, whoever he was; Lazarus stopped, ran his hands over me, let me feel how he'd been missing me. It was all so strong, the way the *before* always is. The ice click-clacking on the plastic porch roof. The way your feet hurt after you stomp them and you're barefoot.

"You know what I want," I said. Said it to his face. He had no idea, of course, but he thought he did. Hoped he did. Kissed me to prove it. "I need a minute first," I told him.

I went into the bathroom. My breathing was off. The huff and the puff of all liars, even those in search of the truth.

I ran the cold water in the tub and took off my clothes. I was standing there, looking in the mirror. My pixie hair had grown in. My skin was pale. I turned off the lights, turned off the tap. I didn't want anything to scare him off, not a wash of light under the door, not any empty tub. I had the marks of the heart monitor on my skin. My heart skipped a beat, but the cardiologist had told me that was now its normal rhythm, abnormal.

I called, "Come in." I said it the way I usually did, like I wanted him, no matter who he was or what he was hiding. By now we had sex perfected, at least for us. Hot but not burning, or burning just enough. I knew to put vinegar on my fever blisters, knew how cold the water had to be for me to take him in my mouth without a scalding, knew him in the dark, the pieces that fit together, the whole man who'd walked with death and had come back to me, for me, with all his secrets.

This is what I knew about him: the cage of his ribs, the rope of his veins, the hardness of his stomach, the hardness of him inside me, the way our mouths fit together, the burning, the heat of the words he said, the rhythm of the sex we had, watery, overflowing, don't ever stop, it's not enough and then it's everything. Was there more to know? I faltered for a moment. I thought of all those women who had sex with monsters in the dark. Men without names who were bears or ogres, men who were enchanted or enslaved. Men covered with sealskin or deerskin, men with claws, men who could not tell a lie, men who could tell nothing but the truth, though it might damn them. Angels disguised, angels exposed; men who had been dead and came back forever changed, forever altered, hiding what they knew. Who they were. The deep inside. The *ever* of the *after*.

He came in the room, already naked. I couldn't see him; I could feel his presence. His flesh, burning. His step on the floor. I was standing with my back against the tile wall. Ready. I suppose he trusted me, as a mole trusts a cat, seeing what awaits only as a shadow, not as a predator who wants what she wants, needs what she needs, has to have it. He got into the tub. I could hear the water; I could hear him settle against the porcelain. Cool against his burning back. Soothing him, probably, like rain on the night when it happened, pouring soaking rain.

The water around him sloshed back and forth. The tiles under my bare feet were cold. So dark I had to feel my way.

Wasn't that part of the story? It is not what you feel or see but what you know in your heart? But my heart was abnormal, the rhythm was off. It thumped against me like a rock against bone. Cold thing, stone thing, thing that would not be red if I ripped it out of my own chest. A piece of ice. Clear. See-through.

I took the candle and put it on the ledge, where there were shampoo bottles, soap. I could feel the bottles with my long clumsy fingers. My bitten nails. The bottles knocked against one another. Time was slow. It was the *before* that I was in, that I was leaving. I could feel myself making my own future, a spider at work on her web. There was a finished woven pattern, one I thought I knew.

When I lit the match, the gleam was so bright I couldn't see anything for a moment. I thought it would be easier this way, less harsh than switching on the light, but I was wrong. I lit the candle and it flared. Blue. Yellow. I was nearly blinded.

"What are you doing?"

I could hear his panic before my eyes adjusted to the light. He was angry. He was shocked. I knew I had to look. Wasn't that the plan? I saw him as he stood, dripping water, lunging forward to grab the candle. Wax fell onto his chest; he didn't seem to notice. He grabbed at the flame, extinguishing it between his fingers. I could smell him burning.

"Well," he said. "This is how it is."

The burning man, cold now. I heard the betrayal. There it was. What had I expected? What had I done?

Now that I had seen what he'd been hiding, I continued to see it through the dark. Branded, is that what they say?

Memory that is stronger than the present, that stays im-
printed behind your eyes, layering itself over everything you
see in the present, in the here and now. I still saw it in the
dark.

Lazarus was marked by the moment of his strike, covered
by what were called lightning figures. I'd read about them
in a book my brother gave me. Usually they were treelike
images imprinted on the body of someone struck by light-
ning. No one was certain if the images were actually trees or
if instead they were some interior path of the veins and ar-
teries. Some experts felt that these designs were shadows
caused by extreme bright light; similar images could be pro-
duced on glass by large charges of electricity. Handprints
appeared on trees, or the perfect shadow of a horse might be
captured on the side of a barn; the last image a person had
seen as he'd been struck by lightning was cast onto his skin,
his soul. All that remained.

"Want a better look? You wanted to see. Look! Go on!"

He was out of the tub, dripping water. He flipped on the
light. I blinked, a cold, untrustworthy fish. I could see my-
self as well. My reflection in the mirror, a pale woman who
was quite capable of repeatedly destroying her own life. I
grabbed a towel, covered myself. I felt like crying. You do
something and you can't go back, can't rewind. I knew that,
didn't I? Ice on the porch, tires on the road, make a wish,
light a candle, ruin your life.

There were the marks of trees, shadow branches up and
down Lazarus's arms. The arms I knew. The rope of veins.

On one arm there was a blackbird, startled, ready to take
flight. And all over there were the wheeling branches, as

though Lazarus was part human and partly made of bark and leaves.

"I'm sorry," I said.

Barely enough. Barely anything. Disloyal, untrustworthy bitch, shivering now, shuddering with the very thought of what I'd done to us. I could never get anything right.

"No, really. Finish it! Look at me."

He grabbed me then. But that wasn't the worst of it, the angry grasp, the hot hands. Far worse was a tone of voice that I hadn't heard before, except in our darkest, deepest moments. No bullshit, no pleasing me, for himself. Just for himself. Whoever that was. Whoever he was.

"Look at it all."

It sounded like a threat. It sounded like the end. And something more. Maybe it was a relief to show someone at last. To turn around and let me see. I did the worst thing when he showed me his back, I made a sound, a gasping, despite my vow to myself to have no reaction. His deepest self, isn't that what I wanted? True self, real self, self you're hiding from the rest of the world.

There was a shadowgraph of a face on his back. Gray and black, the impression of an older man, mouth half open, eyes frightened.

I knew it for what it was right away, expert that I was. There were a hundred ways, and this was one of them. The shadowgraph was of the moment of a man's death.

"Happy?" Lazarus asked me.

I had been — how much so, I had no idea. The *before,* of course. The time I didn't know was the *before,* when I'd had something worthwhile, something I had wanted, something that could be turned to cinders with a single match. How many fairy tales had warned me of this? Keep the light out, have faith, trust in what you feel, not in what you see. Leave the matches at home. Leave it be.

I thought how the meteorologists would love to get their hands on Lazarus. How thrilled they'd be to pose him up against their white screen and photograph him, right, left, naked, one of a kind, piece of art, piece of work, shadow man, death man, my Lazarus, or the Lazarus who had been mine. Terrible time to know the truth, not the truth of him, oh no. The truth of me. But here it was. On the floor. A splash of cold water, a leftover, a strand of red thread that was invisible to me: I didn't know it was love until the moment of bright light. I didn't know what I felt until I went one step beyond it.

"There you have it," Lazarus said. "The real me."

He walked out of the bathroom, slammed the door. I heard the water in the tub, the wind outside. I heard the sound of my own raspy breathing.

I got dressed. I was still shivering. I followed him. I wasn't thinking anymore. That hadn't worked for me. It was hot outside on the porch where he was standing. Too humid to see stars. The odor of red oranges. Do they make perfume out of it? They should. I would buy it and I don't even like cologne. A bottle of oranges, and one of blue ice, and one of tears, and one filled with a potion that was so burning hot when you poured it over your skin you came close to dying. But not really, just hovering above all that was burning, all that was alive.

"You should go and never come back," Lazarus said.

"Tell them if that's what you want to do. Phone the newspaper. I can't stop you. Tell everyone about this damned mark on me."

"It's a shadowgraph. I've read about them. It's probably caused by a brilliant flash of light."

"Is that what it is?" Lazarus almost laughed. But not quite. "Hell, I thought it was my punishment."

"Maybe I'm your punishment," I said.

"Yeah, well, I blame the red dress for everything."

Everything, as in over? *Everything,* as in just beginning? He didn't sound as angry. Only sad. Lost. I knew what that was like. The black trees, the path that can't be found. The ice, falling like stones from above.

The beetles were clicking, and so was my brain. Always my task: undo what has been done. I wanted to whirl time backward, clothes off, lights cut, door open, car on the road.

"I feel him there every minute of every day," Lazarus said. "I know what it is. Whatever you want to call it. It's my punishment all right."

In the story of the fearless boy, the foolish hero played cards with the dead and walked through graveyards without fear, but not even he carried a dead man on his back. The burden of that was an impossible weight. I knew what that was like, too.

Lazarus turned to me. He was barefoot and we were standing on the porch. That alone terrified me. The *then* and the *now* slammed together. His white shirt was wet from his soaking wet skin.

"Aren't you going to ask? You wanted to know, so go ahead. Ask me."

All things happened this way, didn't they? Every story, every life, every coincidence. A left turn instead of a right turn. A stomp of the feet. A wish said aloud. A branch falling from a tree. A storm sweeping in from the east. A butterfly. A candle. A match.

When I didn't ask, he decided to tell me anyway.

"Maybe you shouldn't," I said.

As it turned out, I wasn't so different from my brother when it came to the truth. I felt as though I were about to fall, headfirst, down into the tunnel from which there was no return. *I know I asked, but tell me later, tell me tomorrow or never. That's soon enough.*

Lazarus sat on the top step of the porch. Out in the orchard something was flying around the tops of the trees. There were bats here, too. There was my car, unwashed, dusty, the mileage piling on since I'd begun driving here and back. If I was going to stay, he was going to tell me.

I sat down next to him. I got a splinter — just my luck — but I kept my mouth shut.

Seth Jones, the real Seth Jones, the one with the library cards, had worked on this orchard all his life. He'd been born here and this had been his father's business before him. He was a good son who did as he was told, even after his father had died, even after he himself had gone through middle age. He was so cautious that his life had nearly passed before him and he'd barely noticed. What had he to show for all those years? The oranges he grew were delicious, the land mortgage-free, the workers he hired were honest, and he himself awoke in the mornings, shoulders and legs aching, but alive and well all the same. Maybe that should have been enough.

It wasn't.

Seth Jones, the real one, the true one, wished more than anything that he could change places with someone. He wanted not to be himself. He wanted to travel to countries he'd read about, dreamed of all his life.

One year, and he'd give up half of what he owned.

And then it happened, the way things do, when it's least expected: a temporary worker from the hardware store, a young man of twenty-five, strong, healthy, a lost soul who'd been running his whole life. A foster child, always temporary, always on the move. The young man's shoes were worn down; he had never saved more than a hundred dollars, enough to get to the next town. Twenty-five and he was exhausted. Too many states, too many roads, too many women. He was fed up with life. He dreamed about permanence, stability, trees with roots, land that didn't turn to sand under his feet and slip away.

One afternoon, on a day like any other, he delivered a truckload of mulch, one job of many. Temporary, of course, already fading. But this time he didn't get back in the feed-store truck and drive away. He walked through the orchard, drawn by the scent of oranges and water. He stood at the edge of the pond. He thought about drowning himself, but he knew at the last instant the human spirit always fought to live. He'd spent his whole life traveling, doing as little as possible, getting by. Still, he had his youth, his beautiful face, his strength. Surely this should have been enough.

It wasn't.

Seth Jones saw the stranger fall to his knees. The young man looked as though he was praying, when really he was cursing this world. He was a good man, Seth Jones figured, perhaps sent from above. Surely this was a sign, a man praying for guidance. Seth Jones went right up to the stranger and offered him a bargain no man with just a hundred dollars in his pockets could refuse. One year, not a day more, and in return, half of everything. They shook on it then and there.

The stranger quit his job. He packed up his motel room. He didn't have much, so it didn't take long. On the arranged day, he took a taxi out to the orchard. Everything was set in place: Where to call to hire the farmworkers. Where the checkbook was kept and how to manage Seth Jones's signature. What was a reasonable price for a bushel of oranges, a crate, a truckload. No one would have to see the stranger; he would be Seth Jones while the true Jones was in Italy. That was where his travels would begin. As for the stranger, he felt like someone's son. Maybe that was his dream: a son who had inherited half of everything, as far as the eye could see.

It was a humid day and there were storm clouds. The earth was damp. The air barely moved. So much the better to leave for one man. So much the better to stay for the other.

They were walking through the orchard when it happened. There were blackbirds calling. The air was fragrant. Each man felt as though he'd been given a year to do with as he pleased, the opposite of his own life. The final step of this exchange: they traded shoes. The new man put on the old work boots worn for fifteen years, so comfortable he could wear them from dawn till midnight. Seth Jones put on the younger man's walking shoes, light on his feet, shoes that would carry him far away.

The bad weather must have been a hundred miles off. West. North. Nowhere nearby. Or so it seemed. Then it happened the way things do, when it's least expected. Lightning hit. It tore a hole in the ground. It struck the stranger so hard that his heart stopped. He was floating above himself, and he stayed there, hovering, until he came to himself in the hospital morgue. When he tried to speak, to ask about the other man, smoke came out of his mouth. It was amazing he hadn't been burned alive, that's what he heard the nurses saying. No matter what the experts said about rubber soles, he figured the traded boots were what saved him. But he couldn't figure much beyond that. He was still hovering in some way.

In the hospital he saw the dark, branchlike splotches on his arms. All he could think was that he had to get away. When he stood up from the bath, dripping with ice, he heard them gasp at the marking on his back. It was a burn shaped like a face, someone guessed. A wound shaped like a man. But that wasn't what it was. He knew exactly who he carried: the man to whom he owed a year.

He got dressed and refused any further medical care; he heard those same nurses refer to him as Lazarus. Since he barely remembered his own name, he decided to call himself that as well. What was death like? For him it was a cloud, and he awoke from it clouded still. Where had he been? He had lost himself, and then he was back. If he thought hard, there may have been a battle. He could halfway remember charging through the bath of ice in some way, fighting to come back, slamming down and then arising.

He left the hospital as soon as he could — they had no authority to hold him, he didn't appear to be a danger to himself or others, and he had a bargain to keep. As soon as he returned to the orchard he found the exact spot where he'd been hit. The hole in the ground. The oranges turned red. And then he noticed it, what he was looking for. A pile of ashes. Lazarus got down on his hands and knees and breathed it in. Sulfur and flesh. His partner had been struck and had burst into flame. This was all that was left, a pile of ash and minerals, this and the face imprinted on his back.

Lazarus swept the ashes into a dustpan, then funneled it all into a wooden box he'd found on the bookshelf. He didn't once think of leaving; he kept his part of the bargain. Seth Jones had outlived most of his friends, and Lazarus avoided those Jones had known through his business, hiring workers over the phone, doing his banking by mail and phone. Every night he walked through the orchard to the place where the oranges had turned red. He had made a deal for a year; now he was forced to carry his partner forever more. When the anniversary of that day came, he could feel himself wanting to move on. It was in his blood, that's what he'd discovered. He was never meant to be a settled man. But now he was living another man's life, trapped by circumstance. When did a promise end? With the sort of guilt Lazarus had, the answer seemed to be never.

Lazarus took me back inside; I followed him to the bookshelves. There was the wooden box, carved in Morocco, a death box, a burden.

"Do you think I killed him?" Lazarus said.

It could have been anyone who delivered the mulch that day, but it was him. Anyone who stomped her feet on the porch, but it was me.

I held the wooden box; it was surprisingly heavy, amazingly so. We carried it out through the orchard; it seemed only right that we take Seth Jones with us now. The darkness was sifting through the trees. We went out to the pond, where Jones had first seen Lazarus, the moment when he thought his wish had come true. We left the wooden box and our clothes in a pile and went wading into the water. It was cool and deep. Nights in Florida weren't any more comfortable than the days, only wetter, more humid, closing in, throwing you together. I held Lazarus in my arms. It didn't matter what his name had been; he was Lazarus now. I could feel everywhere he'd been, all those towns, those women, that life. I could feel that he'd made a wish he now regretted, that he'd give anything to have his own shoes back, his own life.

For once in my life I didn't consider the *what had happened* or the *what would be*. None of that. The nowness, the darkness, engulfed us. Two drowning people who loved the feel of water. *Kiss me underwater. Kiss me until I'm gone.* I could feel a shudder go through Lazarus. How odd to have the truth there with us, right there in the black water, drifting. Hot night, beetles flying low, lightning in the distance.

I was far above myself. Floating in the dark. No fear for once in my life. It was not at all what I'd expected. That fearless moment. Salvation where it didn't belong.

I could feel Lazarus shivering in my arms. "It's not your fault," I told him.

And here's the thing I would have never believed about words, my own words, spoken aloud, the ones I said to give him comfort, hope, all those things I'd never believed in: They rescued me.

CHAPTER

FIVE

Gold

I

I'D STAYED AWAY ALL WEEKEND AND ON THE
way home I worried about Giselle. It was Mon-
day, late in the afternoon, nearing suppertime.
The cat would be waiting at the door, desperate
to go out; perhaps she'd already ignored her lit-
ter box, choosing to defecate in one of my shoes
instead, as she often did to vent her anger. I'd
left out a huge bowl of food, but my guilt grew
by the mile. As I was driving home I thought
I heard her mewling, which was impossible.

When I reached the town line, the blue WELCOME TO ORLON sign decorated with oranges and palm trees, I thought I heard Giselle screaming. She'd done that once or twice, when she'd spied another cat through the window, some supposed enemy or lover.

It was only a siren I was hearing — I saw the ambulance in my rearview mirror — but the sound had done its work. My irregular heart was pounding against my ribs. I pulled up in front of my house and got out. It was fairly good weather for Florida, almost crisp, no humidity. No storms. None in sight. All the same, the hair stood up on my arms. I could feel something wrong up and down my spine. I was like a human weather vane, only for tragedy. I had that sour taste in my mouth and I hadn't even made a wish.

I ran up to the door and let Giselle out. She was angry with me, had her haughty expression on, her tail up; she went past me and jumped around in the weeds. She turned her back to me to pee. She was a private creature and I respected that. She held a grudge; I respected that, too.

I wanted to go inside, take a shower, put on some clean clothes, reconsider my life. I thought perhaps I'd discovered the difference between love and obsession. Only one of them puts you in jeopardy. I felt like a gambler who had only just realized how much there was to lose. Everything seemed different. The steps I took, the scratchy weeds against the bare skin of my leg, my cat mewing.

Giselle trotted past me to the door. She had something in her mouth. I hoped it was a bird, not another poor mole. I chased after her. She shook her prey back and forth. It was brown, whatever she'd caught: feathers or fur, I couldn't tell.

Giselle rubbed back and forth against my legs, then deposited her catch at my feet. No longer angry that I'd been gone so long, proud of herself. She had given me a gift. I suppose she was my pet — and I, her what? Surely not her keeper. Perhaps I was her pet in return. Her little murderess. Her darling dear.

I bent down, cautious. The thing at my feet didn't seem familiar. And then, it was.

It was a leather glove. When I peered inside I saw flecks of gold.

I ran back across the lawn. I found the other glove under the hedge. It was curled up like something broken, a leaf, a bird, a mole, a heart.

Monday. The day after I was supposed to have met Renny to finish his architecture project. I'd forgotten.

I went into my house, through the living room, into the kitchen. The Doric temple, unfinished. The gloves on the lawn. My irregular heart. My greedy self. My wish that he would disappear.

I heard someone call my name. The voice was unfamiliar. I charged back through the house and saw a young woman on my front porch.

"Hullo," she called.

I peered through the screen door.

"I had a message from Renny Mills," the woman said. She was young, blond, wearing jeans and a T-shirt. She looked somewhat familiar.

"You have a message for me?"

"No. For me. Renny left me a note to meet him here. We were in art history class together in the spring."

Iris McGinnis.

She laughed, nervous. She was thin and pale, with a sweet expression. "He said he had a present for me. I don't know why he'd want to give me anything."

Because he's madly in love with you, idiot, I wanted to say. I opened the screen door. She was very young. Nineteen, perhaps. I had a terrible sinking feeling.

"He's been making you something," I said.

"Me?" Iris laughed, and the sound was like water. Maybe that was what he'd fallen in love with, that sound.

"But he's not here."

"Okay, well, can you have him call me?"

Iris wrote down her phone number on the back of a piece of notepaper.

"I'll be home all day. Studying. I'm not as smart as Renny is. He got an A in the class we took together and I was lucky to get a C. I'll just wait for his call."

"Sure," I said.

"I can't believe he has a present for me." She had green eyes, I noticed. She was pretty in a pale, sweet way.

When Iris left I phoned Renny's dorm. Someone answered and, when I asked for him, said, "You haven't heard?"

I felt panic-stricken. I had the gloves on my bureau. My hair was sticking up as though I'd been shocked.

"What did he do?" I asked. I knew it was something bad, something desperate, a monster's attempt to tear off his skin, an angel's attempt to rise.

I pieced it together from that initial call and then a call to my brother. Everyone in the Science Center knew. Renny had walked into Acres' Hardware Store and taken a hatchet from the wall. He'd been calm and cheerful; no one had even noticed him. Now there was so much blood on the floor of the hardware store that new oak planks would have to be installed. Renny would have surely bled to death if the manager of the paint department, the man who'd been attacked by the bulldog, hadn't taken a lifesaving course. The manager was a quick thinker; he'd been so ever since his own attack. He jumped over the counter and made a tourniquet out of the strings of his Acres' Hardware apron.

Because of the incident, and the university's liability, the lightning-strike study was to be disbanded. There hadn't been enough psychological supervision, that's what Renny's parents were saying, and it was rumored that a lawsuit loomed. Orlon University had no vested interest in the study. Twelve years of research was to be poured down the drain; all those photographs of us, the charts of our poor health, would be shredded now.

Everyone I spoke to wondered why on earth someone would commit such a horrible act, right there in the hardware store on a perfectly ordinary day. But I understood why Renny had tried to cut off his hand. I was sure that when he walked past the girls at the checkout counter and smiled at them, they hadn't bothered to smile back; like all those students at Orlon who walked right past him, they most likely hadn't even seen him. Renny walked through the store, the invisible man, with one thought in mind. I knew him well enough to know that. A single desire, his defining secret: he wanted to be human.

I went immediately to the hospital, found the intensive

care unit, and talked myself into the waiting area. I knew a few of the nurses, and I was clearly upset and involved. I wasn't family, and therefore couldn't see the patient, but they would allow me to wait. For what, I wasn't certain. I sat down on one of the hard plastic chairs.

I suppose I was easy to pick out if someone had heard about me: lightning-strike victim, distraught friend, fellow monster in disguise. A teenaged girl came to sit next to me. "You're Renny's friend," she said. She introduced herself as his sister, Marina.

"Will he recover?" I asked.

"It's not as bad as it sounds." Marina had a soft voice, like Renny's. She wore a black velvet headband that pushed back her hair. I suppose she was a redhead, but her hair looked white to me. A little old woman, concerned about her brother. He'd told me she was the smart one. The favorite. "They had to sew the hand back on, reattach all the nerves. He may not feel anything. Or maybe he'll just feel less. But mostly he lost a lot of blood."

"I was supposed to help him with a project. That's why this happened. I forgot all about it."

I felt that I should get down on my knees and beg Marina's forgiveness. I should cut out my heart and place it on the vinyl tiles of the floor.

"The Doric temple? It wasn't for class. He was already failing when he asked you for help. He wanted to create something to give to some girl he's in love with."

"Iris," I said.

"Is she worth it?" Marina asked.

"I don't know. I only met her today."

Renny's parents had gone to collect his personal belongings from his dorm room. They were meeting with their lawyer as soon as they got back to Miami. They might not have appreciated someone from the lightning-strike study visiting Renny, but Marina took me to see him.

"It's not that my parents wouldn't like you, it's just that they're protecting him from the world. Parents." Marina shrugged. "They want the best and do the worst. I'm just holding my breath till I'm on my own."

When we reached Renny's room, I peered in from the doorway. There he was. Under the sheets. Eyes closed. There was some machine that made a sound like snow falling.

"Knock, knock," Marina called. No reply. "Demerol," she whispered to me. "He's been out for a while."

She led me in to see him. The room was darkened and we could see the flecks of gold in his hands. He had no idea of how beautiful he was, none at all.

We went to stand by the bed.

"It's okay," Marina said. "You can talk to him."

"Hey." My voice sounded faint. It echoed as though I were far away when I was right there. "It's me."

Renny opened his eyes. He didn't turn away from me the way I thought he would. That was something.

I saw a line of red along his left arm — the line where they'd sewed him together. I saw it — that amazing, sharp, and painful red. It had been so long since I had seen the color that I was nearly blinded. I had forgotten its intensity.

"I wanted to be normal," Renny said. "I wanted to feel things."

"You've got a funny way of being normal," I said.

His parents would take him home, and Marina would bring him cups of tea and bowls of broth until he recovered. One day someone would see him for who he really was and fall in love with him.

"What should I do with your project?" I asked.

He smiled. He had a great smile. "Not much call for Doric temples. Throw the fucker out."

"Actually Iris came for it."

"Who?" he said.

We both laughed at that. Girl of his dreams. Maybe it would be better now for her to stay there.

"I was a lousy friend," I said.

Renny was a gentleman, even now, drugged-up and in pain. "There's worse," he said.

"Who, a mass murderer?"

"Me," he said.

I leaned down and kissed Renny's forehead. "Thanks," he said to me. I think that's what he said. He was already falling back asleep.

"He's tired," Marina said.

Her hair was red, I could see that now. I blinked and was still stunned by how beautiful the color was. When I got my bearings, I wrote down my address. "Will you let me know how he's doing?"

I felt that I had dreamed him up — Renny was that honest and that true.

"Do you think it's possible for him to be happy?" she asked.

She wasn't much more than a girl.

"I think anything is possible," I said. It sounded as though I meant it.

I LEFT, BACK INTO THE HEAT OF THE DAY. I WAS WALKING across the parking lot to my car, thinking about love and why it mattered. It was an idea, wasn't it? Nothing real, nothing lasting, nothing to live or die for. In all the talks I'd had with Jack Lyons, I'd never once asked him what he thought about love. I hadn't wanted to know.

The clouds were moving quickly in the sky. There was so much blue and there was the color I'd missed the most moving across all that blue. So startling. So alive. It was a cardinal flying above the treetops. I stood there with a hand over my eyes. After so much time, even the smallest amount of that color hurt my retinas. I think I felt tears.

I heard something. Renny's sister running after me.

"Hold on," she called.

I turned and waited for her to catch up.

"Renny said you'd take care of this."

Marina held out her hands and I held out mine. She turned over the little mole Renny had rescued from the cat. It felt like a glove, a leaf, a wish.

"What's going to happen to him?" I said.

"I'll take care of Renny. When he's better he'll go to the University of Miami. Art history. Or did you mean the mole?"

I hadn't, but I supposed I should be interested in the poor thing; he was my responsibility now.

"If you can't find grubs or earthworms, Renny said to feed it American cheese and lettuce. Twice a day."

It was nothing I wanted. Nothing I cared about. But mine all the same. I held the mole up and looked into its blind face. And then I realized what love did. It changed your whole world. Even when you didn't want it to.

ON THE WAY TO MY BROTHER'S HOUSE I SAW FLASHES OF red everywhere. I suppose I was recovering. Or maybe I was hallucinating, imagining what I wanted most to see. The sign on the mini-mart flashed so deeply crimson it took my breath away. Had such ridiculous things been beautiful before and I simply hadn't noticed? I stopped, pulled into the lot, went inside the market, to the fruit aisle. Wrapped lettuce, cucumbers, peaches, lemons, and then, at last, a single pale apple, blushed on one side as if filled with life, with blood. I bought the apple and ate it in my car. It was delicious, all the more so because of its color. Sitting in my parked car, I felt absurdly alone without Renny. I'd gotten involved, even though I'd known it was always a mistake.

I drove along idly until I was on my brother's street. This was often where the story went in a fairy tale. Sun and moon, brother and sister, the guardian and the guarded, opposites who gave each other form, guided each other until they stumbled home. Ned was at the university; I knew an emergency meeting of the lightning-research group had been called. There was a great deal of worry about the lawsuit Renny's family was threatening. None of the experts had offered him counseling, taken note that he might be unbalanced. Well, weren't we all? It was true for all of the members of our study group. We'd been turned inside out, picked up and dropped down, flattened, wounded, torn apart. I'd seen the Naked Man several times, wandering through the park, stopping to throw tennis balls for other people's retrievers and poodles. I'd seen the young girl with the mismatched socks at the coffee shop in town, her hand held over a tabletop, trying to make a spoon turn in a circle.

Frankly, I thought if Renny's family sued anyone, it should be me. Ignorant, selfish, greedy, blind, the friend who wasn't there. Oh, definitely, it should be me, although what they might take in reparations was minimal: my cat, my car, my future, my past.

I got out of the car onto my brother's street, and tossed the apple core away. I suppose seeing Renny's sister and her devotion had made me think of Ned. I'd been a terrible sister; I should have told him about Nina and *A Hundred Ways to Die*. Now, I knocked on the door. The car wasn't in the driveway. Maybe Nina walked to her classes; the mathematics building wasn't far. It was such a beautiful day. It was getting dark earlier. That was the only thing that was the same here as it was in New Jersey. By now the maples would have begun to turn red with the first rush of cooler weather. Here there was just a slow bluing of everything. Birds sang in the darkening sky, and a few palm fronds, ones that had turned dry with the heat, rattled and shook in the breeze.

I made my way through the hedge of gardenia and peered into the window. A white sofa. A framed red heart on the wall. Nina opened the door and stood there. I think I'd woken her. Her hair was mussed. Her eyes were foggy. I wasn't quite certain whether she recognized me. Even when she spoke, she wasn't connecting in any way. I might have been the paperboy or a door-to-door salesman.

"Your brother's not here. He's at the Science Center. There's some sort of alleged crisis."

"Yeah, well, a friend of mine tried to cut off his hands. He was in the lightning study."

"Some people make their own grief."

Nina eyed me meaningfully. So it was true. She didn't like me. She was wearing a smock with paint smeared over it. I noticed she didn't invite me in.

"Are you painting?"

"Yes. Obviously." The color was yellow. I could see that on her fingers, her blue jeans.

"Do you have any American cheese?" I said.

Nina laughed. A funny, broken sound, but light, like chimes. "You're here for cheese?"

I took the mole out of my pocket. Nina took a step back, stunned.

"Jeez." She nearly laughed.

"I'm taking care of it for my friend."

Nina opened the door, and I followed her inside. We went through the living room, past the heart on the wall, into the kitchen. I could smell paint. I liked the smell: something covering up something, something brand-new.

I sat down while Nina rummaged through the fridge. I put the mole down and stared at it. It didn't move. I hoped it wasn't going to die on me.

"Please don't put that thing on the table," Nina said when she approached with a packet of orange cheese.

I lifted the mole, set my backpack on the table, then placed the mole atop it.

"Some things aren't meant to be pets." Nina sat down at the table. She gazed at the mole. "Fair creature who cannot see or hear or want or need." She looked at me. "It doesn't seem to like the cheese."

She went to the pantry for some of the food my brother left out for bats at their feeder in the yard. Fruit and veggies pureed and stored in a jar. I took a spoon of the mush and placed it in a little plate. The mole took a mouthful of what appeared to be smushed grape. I had the book in my backpack. *A Hundred Ways to Die.* The mole was probably sitting on it right now. I saw the pulse at Nina's throat, delicate, pale pink.

"What is it like to love someone?" I asked.

Nina laughed. At any rate, she made a noise. "Ridiculous question. There are countless answers to that one."

"Then to you. What does it mean to you?"

I could see into the yard from where I was sitting. The sky was salmon, then gray, then dark and deep, a bluish color, one I hadn't seen before. Nothing like New Jersey. Something infinite, hot, faraway.

Nina was gazing out at the yard.

"I thought you loved him," I said.

Nina turned back to me, surprised.

"Ned," I said. "I thought you truly loved him."

Nina glared and went to the sink. She just stood there. Didn't bother to turn on the water. *Oh,* she said. I think that's what she said.

"Look, I was there in the library," I told her. "That's why

I'm saying this to you. You think I want to get involved? I didn't want to see you, but I did. I know you withdrew *A Hundred Ways to Die*. If Ned knew what you were planning, it would destroy him."

Nina laughed, but the sound was dry. Nothing funny here.

"I'm the one destroyed," she said.

"You're planning to kill yourself."

"Oh, far worse."

Nina turned and left the room, so I followed her. I went down the dark hall. Nina was standing in the study, now cleared of furniture. She had painted one wall yellow. She hadn't bothered to turn on the overhead light, but the room was glowing. Yellow did that. This yellow.

"Nice color," I said.

Nina sat down on the floor, legs crossed. She'd covered the carpet with a drop cloth. I sat across from her and watched her cry. When she was done she wiped her eyes with the palms of her hands.

"You want to know what love is? It's the thing that ruins you."

Nina looked straight at me. She reached out and for a second I thought she meant to hit me. I wouldn't have blamed her if she had. I was rude, asking too many questions, insinuating myself where I wasn't wanted, spying on her. Instead, she took my hand and put it on her stomach. She was farther along than anyone would have guessed. She'd kept her secret well. I could feel the baby moving.

"This isn't ruin. This is wonderful. Why would you ever take out that book?" I said.

I looked right into her, and I saw what love was to her.

"The book was for him. In case it got too hard for him and he didn't want to live through it. In case I couldn't stand to watch his pain."

I didn't want to understand what she was talking about. It was ruin; she was right. It was opening yourself to be destroyed. One minute you have everything. And then the next it's all gone.

This was that time.

"He has pancreatic cancer. He wants to work as long as he can, which they say is less than a month. The baby will be here after the first of the year. The book was in case he wanted it. To go as he chose. It's his right, after all. It's his life. But then I couldn't go through with it. Even a minute less time of him in the world would be too hard. I returned it."

Nina's face was blotchy; the rims of her eyes were a pale red. Even I could see that color.

"I can paint the room and you can watch me," I said.

"We can paint tomorrow," Nina suggested. "At least there's time for that."

We sat there in the dark, holding hands. And then I knew the answer to my question.

This is what it was.

11

As soon as it was strong enough, I set the mole free in the yard at dusk. I put it on the grass near the hedge and it disappeared. One minute it was there, the next it was gone. I suppose this was familiar territory, the scent of the hibiscus, the feel of the dried grass. The mole didn't leave any tracks; it just vanished.

I thought about the way old blind women in stories found their lost loves and recognized them even though fifty or a hundred years had passed, even if their husbands or lovers had been turned into stags or monsters. I thought about how the familiar imprinted itself on you — a hedge, a scent, a touch. If someone had taken a photograph of Lazarus and me together and pinned it to a wall, anyone who'd seen it would have thought, *They aren't meant for each other. They don't belong together.* So we didn't take any photographs. I had questioned how it was possible for this man to love me all along, but I had finally begun to understand the reason: I knew him. If he came to me as a bear or a deer, I would still know him. If I were blind, if it was at dusk, if a hundred years had passed, I'd still know.

That couldn't be taken away, despite ruin, despite time.

That night I drove out and we went walking through the orchard in the dark. During the day, the workers Lazarus had hired called to one another and the picking machinery was noisy. But at night you could hear every breath, every beetle.

I told Lazarus about my brother. I looked for blame everywhere: if we'd never lived in New Jersey, if we'd breathed different air, if he'd had a different diet, had never come to Florida, if we'd had different parents, grandparents, a different genetic makeup, maybe his cancer wouldn't have happened. There was another, earlier theory my brother had told me about, the uncertainty principle, a theorem that predated and informed chaos theory. The simple fable to illustrate it explains that a cat will live or die depending on the utterly random decay of a single atom. And so it was for Ned. One cell affected another; one bloody random cell utterly defined everything. Why it should happen to him, it was impossible to know. There were not hundreds of possible answers, but thousands. All unknowable and random. All out of reach.

"What do I do for him?" I asked Lazarus. I thought a dead man would know such things.

Lazarus laughed. He rarely did. "You'd have to ask him. It's different for everyone."

"If you had a few weeks to live, how would you want to live it?"

I wanted him to say, *Like this, walking with you in the dark.* I wanted him to help me through, but Lazarus wasn't like that. It wasn't his fault. He was too trapped in his own life to really think about someone else's.

"If it was me, I'd want to be free. Like I used to be. I thought my life was nothing, until I lost it. If people knew who I am, they'd want to know what happened to Seth, and I doubt they'd believe me. They'd think I killed him, took his money. So here I am. Stuck."

Trapped in the wrong shoes, in the woods where every path led back to the exact same place. I understood how Lazarus might want to be in his own skin again. This wasn't his life. That was why I wanted to remember everything about this night. I was going to lose it, all of it, I could tell standing there. Sooner or later. Ruin. I looked at every leaf, every star.

"I think I'll be found out anyway," Lazarus said. "I think people are starting to realize I'm not the right Seth Jones."

The feedstore had balked the last time he'd tried to make a transaction over the phone. Why didn't he ever come in to place his order? He'd had to talk to the manager, who had known the real Seth Jones and who said, "What's wrong with you, Jonesy? Frog in your throat?"

"Flu, damn near pneumonia," Lazarus had answered. But he was worried. The year of their bargain had passed. Come and gone. He'd been thinking about leaving, and now he thought harder. Maybe he would already be gone if he hadn't made a promise to the old man. If I hadn't driven out, wearing that red dress. Filled my mouth with ice and kissed him.

Feel lucky for what you have when you have it. Isn't that the point? Happily ever after doesn't mean happy forever. The *ever after,* what precisely was that? Your dreams, your life, your death, your everything. Was it the blank space that went on without us? The forever after we were gone?

So now. So here. So him. The heat, the black night, the stars, the moment, the *ever after* floating inside of us.

There was something wrong with the crop. That was the other reason he didn't feel right about taking off. He led me out to the place where lightning had struck. A few cars passed on the road, but no one paid any attention. We were a man and a woman walking through the past. The hole in the ground had widened greatly, the earth was falling in on itself, inch by inch, revealing a rocky, hard core. At the outer circle more and more trees were dying. One day they were filled with fruit, the next they were leafless and black.

Around the circle, there were still a few trees with red or-
anges. Now I saw it. Not icefruit or snowballs, but ruby red.
Red worlds, red globes, beautiful in the dark. How could I
have been so stupid to ignore everything I'd had in my life?
The color red alone was worth kingdoms.

"I want to pick some," I said.

We took one of the ladders and set it against a tree; I
climbed up and tossed the oranges to Lazarus.

"Enough," he said. "We'll never eat them all."

But I couldn't stop. More and more. I'd been starving; not
anymore.

It was a cool night, but these oranges kept in heat. Little
globes of burning sunlight. We carried the basket together.
For this one night, in love, in love. Everything meant some-
thing to us. Black sky, black trees, red oranges, sweet smell
of the earth, the heat when he whispered to me, the sound of
our feet on the dirt paths, the sprinkler system switching on,
water falling.

We took off our clothes in the orchard and went under
the sprinklers. In the night air, under water, we could em-
brace each other any way we wanted to. There was no one
for miles around. No one else at all. I loved the way he felt,
so real, so *here,* so *now.* I loved his muscles under his skin, the
heat from his body, the way his kisses burned. I loved the
way it hurt, the way it made me know I was alive, *now* and
in the *ever after,* seeing red, wanting to go down on my hands
and knees, not caring if there was another person in the uni-
verse. No wonder people did this however and with whom-
ever; with strangers, in parking lots, desperate, greedy;
joined together, you can imagine you're not alone, the only

one. So different, because when you are in love, that's the joke: you feel your aloneness so deeply it hurts. *When I'm not with you.*

"Stop thinking," Lazarus said to me.

I was freezing, without clothes, soaked by all that cold water, the sprinklers, the starlight, the *now, the now.*

I kissed him and let the rest fall away. He sat on the ground, pulled me down. I was in his lap with him inside me, able to look right into his eyes, the way they were like ashes. I ran my hands down his back. I felt everything. There wasn't another man, shadowgraph or not. It was just him. Skin, muscles, bones, heart, blood, red, heat.

I just let go. I gave up, gave in: I stopped fighting being alive.

It was the time I would remember, more than the fish, tub, ice, pond, fast, hard, slow, baby; it was this, drowning while I knew he was thinking about leaving. We were a human example of chaos theory, thrown together by circumstance. We didn't belong together, I knew that. But for one night we were perfect.

When we went back to the house I took a hot shower. I was shivering, even when I got dry and had dressed. I took a sweater from the bureau drawer in the bedroom, then went into the kitchen. Lazarus was wearing the clothes he'd had on before; he still had mud on him. He was sitting at the table. He looked at me when I came into the room. I could tell from his expression that there was always a price to pay. The ruin. The sorrow. The *ever after.*

"Without you I would have been completely alone," he said.

I looked at his mouth, the bones of his face, his ashy eyes, his wide hands, and the way his veins roped through his arms. Blue and red. Alive. I looked hard. I wanted to remember that he'd wanted me once. I put this moment into the *ever after,* the core of everything I'd ever known.

He had cut all of the oranges I'd picked in half. It looked as though there was blood on the table, but it was only juice. These were the oranges that had been bringing the most profit at market. People liked how rare they were, the splash of color in a fruit bowl, in their mouths. He'd been getting double the price, but not anymore.

The ones he'd cut in half were black in the center. All that sweet red fruit that tasted like a surprise, that was gone. The oranges were rotting from the inside out. I'd heard about such occurrences. A tree that had been hit would stand for months and no one would guess it was dying at its center until it fell to the ground. Effects took time; you looked away, you thought you were safe, then they happened. Before you knew it, everything had changed.

The story is always about searching for the truth, no matter what it might bring. Even when nothing was what it appeared to be, when everything was hidden, there was a center not even I could run from: who I truly was, what I felt, what I was deep inside.

Hope

I

RENNY'S FAMILY HAD BROUGHT A LAWSUIT against Orlon University. Ever careful and prudent, the university protected itself, like a creature that could only think to sting. My brother's research was gone. Someday someone else would collect similar information and would interview lightning victims, photograph them against a white wall, but that would be then. Not now. In the now that we lived in, everything went through the shredder and was turned to dust.

I had thought of a way to give my brother some of the life he wanted to live. Something that might please him, interest him, something to remember in the *ever after*. I asked Nina, and she agreed, so I phoned my brother at work. I hadn't seen him or spoken to him since Nina had told me. My brother and I weren't exactly used to the truth. So I dodged it a bit longer.

"Before they shred it, get the Dragon's file," I told Ned.

I had managed to gain a referral from Craven, my cardiologist, so that I could speak with the attending cardiologist in Jacksonville. When I asked about the Dragon, the cardiologist told me the old fellow came back stronger both times he'd been struck by lightning. He was an ox of a man who still walked ten miles a day.

"We ran tests on him. He said he was too old to give us more than one day to study him. Said it was a waste of time. According to the facts of his condition, he should have stayed dead. His heartbeat was less than ten beats a minute, slower than a bear in hibernation. He was eighty-seven years old when his second strike took place. He was knocked flat on his back and received so many volts it was immeasurable. Then he got up and had lunch. He refused all medical care, and as far as we know, he's the healthiest old bastard in the state. Go figure."

"You want me to steal his file?" my brother said now when I phoned him. "As in just take it?"

"Right now."

Ned laughed; he seemed pleased at the idea of a small criminal act committed against the university.

"If I get caught, I'll say you're the mastermind."

I was nervous about seeing Ned. I thought I'd say something stupid. Wouldn't that be just like me. I figured a public place might be best; with people around, I might behave myself. I might not cry.

I met him at the diner in town for breakfast and he handed over the file.

"The Dragon's an anomaly. One of a kind. Even if he'd talked to us, he would have done nothing for our study. He's what people doing research call an 'anecdote' — a great story, but meaningless in the greater scheme of research. Just a lucky old bastard. And since there's no longer a study, it doesn't really matter."

"Let's go see him," I said.

Ned had ordered a single scrambled egg and toast. He hadn't even eaten half.

"We'll be back by tonight," I assured him.

"We never had anyone go out there and examine him. We can't even be sure he's still alive. Plus . . ." He played with his food. "Plus, I'm not feeling so great."

"I asked Nina and she said you could go."

"You asked Nina? What am I, five years old? Do I need permission?"

Leave it to me to say the wrong thing. I signaled the waitress and ordered rice pudding and tea. When I turned back, my brother was cleaning his glasses on his shirt. I saw that the skin under his eyes was scaly with rosy patches.

"She told you," Ned said. He didn't seem particularly angry, only disappointed.

"I sort of forced her to, Ned. I mean, I'm your sister. I should know if you're ill."

"Like I know about your life? Let's face it, we don't even know each other."

"Ned," I said. "I'm so sorry."

"That's exactly why I didn't want it this way!" He really was angry. "No sorrowful 'Ned.' Don't say it that way. No bullshit. No standing on the porch. I really couldn't stomach that."

Now I was pissed. "What's that supposed to mean?"

"It means I'm not coming home, either. Don't wait for me. Don't think anything's going to turn out differently. Don't think there's something you can do to prevent it. And for once in your life, don't think it's about you."

I got up and went outside. The heat was crazy. I felt as though I were suffocating. Melting, but melting into what? I had wanted to give my brother a gift. Do something he'd been wanting to do. A single memorable day. Stupid, as usual. Mistake, naturally.

My brother had paid the bill and now he came outside. We didn't look at each other. Finally Ned spoke. "Am I supposed to apologize for dying?"

"Yes. Apologize. How fucking dare you?"

I was too loud. My eyes were hot. I really might have been going crazy. I glared at him. I hated my brother. I thought if I was left behind again, I would break into pieces. I thought about how everything came too late.

My brother and I stood there in the heat. Pissed. Sweating. Older than we'd ever thought we'd be. This wasn't our natural habitat. I wanted to rewind things. Maybe Ned did, too. He'd calmed down.

"I heard you helped paint the room for the baby," he

said. More neutral, cheerful territory, if it weren't so tragic.

"I would have preferred red. I'm seeing some shades of it now."

"Okay. I apologize," my brother said. "It's all my fault. Fuck me with my fucking goddamn cancer."

Now he was the one to turn away. Ruin. The word I despised. It was happening to him.

"We'll just have to turn you around, so Death isn't standing at your feet. Then he won't be able to take you."

Ned laughed. He pulled himself together. Faced me again. Once you knew, you saw it. His face looked different. Thin. Tired.

"There's no fooling that son of a bitch." My brother shook his head, amused. "I love that story."

"Why? It's terrible."

"It's true."

We both thought about that.

"Well, in the story Death is tricked."

"Only twice, little sister. Then he gets what belongs to him."

"The Dragon's still alive and he tricked Death twice."

"So, we're off to see the Dragon. Is that why? Find out the tricks of the trade? It ain't gonna work, baby girl."

"We're just going," I said. "Think of it as a field trip."

"You're not the only one who knows a secret. Nina told me. You've got yourself a boyfriend."

"Now we're even," I said.

Did I sound jaunty? Did I sound as though I could make it through the conversation?

"Yeah, you get to fall in love; I die. Very even."

I thought that the people inside the diner were in a different universe, one where there was sustenance, hope, good health. The heat could wear a person out. Maybe there was nothing I could do for Ned. I was ready to back down. Then my brother turned to me.

"Your car or mine?"

"Seriously?"

"How many times do you get to see a dragon?"

It took two hours to get up north; I drove and Ned slept the whole time. Nina had told me he'd tried chemo when he'd first been diagnosed, but it had made him so sick he hadn't been able to work; the doctors had agreed that the treatment was doing more harm than good. He was trying to last until January, when the baby would be born. It seemed unlikely that he would.

"Jesus, I'm drooling," Ned said when he woke up.

We got to the outskirts of Jacksonville at noon. Hotter here. Impossible, but true. The air conditioner of my car started to sputter. Overworked, pissy. We pulled into a gas station and I got out to check the directions I'd gotten off the record from the cardiologist who'd treated the Dragon. I'd begged him, as a matter of fact. I told him I was a lightning-strike survivor who needed hope. He had no reason to disbelieve me.

There were several back roads we'd have to take and I worried that the ride was too bumpy for Ned.

Every once in a while I would look at him.

"Stop that. Just concentrate on driving. Fuck it," he added when we went into a ditch. There was a trailer and a fellow sitting outside. "Pull over," Ned said.

He got out and spoke with the elderly man in the lawn chair. It looked as if this fellow had the same lawn chair I had. Acres' Hardware. I guess it was a statewide chain. Ned and the old man shook hands and spoke a few words, then Ned came back to the car. "Five miles up. But the Dragon won't talk to us without an introduction, so says the gentleman in the lawn chair."

"What does that asshole know?"

I noticed the fellow was locking his door, heading for our car.

"That asshole's the Dragon's son."

"Hey," our new companion said as he got in the backseat. "I'm Joe." He was about seventy years old. Minimum. "I'll take you to see my dad."

"We never had a father," Ned said as I got back to driving. "Well, we had one, but he took off."

"Son of a bitch," Joe said, sympathetic to our plight. "My dad is right up the road."

"Now I'm dying and leaving my own kid before he's born," Ned said.

My throat was drying up. That kind of talk could make you cry; you had to concentrate and start counting right away, or you'd lose it.

"That's different." Joe had lit a cigarette; I kept my mouth shut, even though it would be weeks before I could get the stink out of my car. "That's not abandonment. You don't want to leave, so you'll probably linger."

"Linger?" Ned said.

"In spirit."

Shut up, old man, I wanted to say. I strained to be polite. This was too difficult. This couldn't be about Ned. "We don't believe in that."

Joe leaned forward. "What do you believe in?"

We thought that over until Joe shouted, "Pull over now!"

We did, and nearly got stuck in a meadow of saw grass. It was sloppy, muddy stuff, but I found a dry place to park. There was the Dragon's house, a cottage that looked a little like mine. When I'd stopped at the gas station I'd bought chips and soda. A little refreshment. Joe went on ahead to make sure his father was presentable, then he stuck his head back out the door.

"Come on," Joe said.

"You're giving a ninety-year-old man soda pop and potato chips?" my brother said.

"Oh, shut up." I grinned. God, it was hot. "What should I bring? Pablum?"

"What do you want to bet he has no air conditioner," Ned said.

At least there was an overhead fan, but it seemed to be spinning in slow motion. The Dragon of Jacksonville didn't look much older than his son. Pretty spry, actually.

"You tracked me down," the Dragon said. "I hope you brought me something to make this visit worth my while."

He was sitting in an easy chair made out of fake leather. A good-looking old man. Still had his hair, lots of it, white.

I held up the chips and pop, and the Dragon nodded, pleased. He suggested that Joe serve us all drinks with ice.

"What about you?" he said to my brother. Ned looked at

me. He hadn't thought to bring anything. "That's a nice watch," the Dragon said.

Ned smiled, unclasped it, and handed it over.

"Tells good time," Ned said.

"There's no time like the present," the Dragon said.

It was a joke, so we laughed appreciatively. We had Coke with ice and sat on uncomfortable stools. It was sweltering. The Dragon pulled up his undershirt and showed us where the lightning had struck first.

"Dead for fourteen minutes and forty-five seconds," Joe said proudly. "I timed him."

Then Joe took off his father's slippers and showed us the Dragon's feet. They were curled up like hooves. "Arthritis," Joe said. "Runs in the family." He showed us the marks on the soles.

"The lightning hit a tree, ricocheted, went along the ground, and struck him dead for fifty-five minutes flat the second time."

"What was it like?" I asked the Dragon.

"Funny thing. It was just like this," the Dragon said. "Like sitting here with you. Soon you'll go away. That's what it was. One minute it was one thing, the next it was something else."

"And how did you come back?"

Ned elbowed me. I suppose I was being rude. But there wasn't much time, was there? That's why we were here.

"If I knew that, I wouldn't have bought a plot in the cemetery the very next week. It was just a preview, not the whole show. I'm back because I'm back." The Dragon took a gulp of soda pop. "Now I'd like to ask you something. Maybe you know — is there a reason for everything?"

We all looked at my brother, the scientist, for an answer.

"Just because we don't know it or understand it doesn't mean there's not a reason," Ned said.

"There you go." The Dragon was pleased with that response. "My sentiments exactly."

He held out my brother's watch. It was an old Rolex. Nina had gotten it for him on their tenth anniversary. It had cost a fortune and she had scoured antiques shops in Orlando till she found the right one.

"Want it back?"

Ned shook his head. "No time like the present," he said.

"Then I'm going to show you a secret. You paid for it. You deserve it. Just don't go telling your cronies. I'm not a sideshow."

It took quite a while to walk down the road a piece. "Down the road a piece" was far, the way things always were in Florida. Ned was tired and the Dragon was slow, especially in the soppy saw grass.

"We're going to wind up getting ticks," I said. "Fleas. Poison something. Oak or ivy."

"Do you smell it?" My brother had stopped and took a deep breath. "This is where the salt water meets up with the stream and mixes."

It was salty and fetid both. Underneath it all was a sweetness. Here we were, older than our mother had been, wandering through the muck on a day when it was over a hundred degrees, following two old men through the swamp.

"I just want you to know: if I see an alligator, I'm turning around."

Ned laughed. "But snakes don't count, right?" My brother nodded, and when I saw a slithery thing in the grass, I grabbed his arm. "Harmless," he said. "Milk snake."

I realized then that my brother seemed happy. The place where his watch had been shone, white skin, naked, new. His khaki pants were streaked with mud and saw grass.

"Okay, here we are," the Dragon said. "I can spit fire, you know that, right?"

Well, I'd seen Lazarus set fire to paper, burn me with a kiss — I thought I was ready. But the Dragon actually spit, and where it landed flames rose out of the saw grass. Joe ran over and stomped them out.

"Well, that's physiologically impossible," my brother said. All the same, he sounded excited. He looked wide-awake.

"So I've been told," the Dragon said. "And I figured out how you can stop it." The Dragon reached into his pocket and brought out something that looked like a tulip bulb. "Straight garlic. Takes the fire right out of a person. But I don't want to do that now, 'cause I'm going to show you something worth seeing. You didn't come all this way for me. Now promise you'll keep this to yourselves."

My brother crossed his heart. My eyes were burning. I thought of him in New Jersey, watching the bats in the sky. I thought about the colony of ants he'd had to leave behind when we moved in with our grandmother. I didn't care about the things I couldn't take with me, but my brother was different; after my grandmother put her foot down, Ned went out behind her house and set the ants free. I watched from the bedroom window. I never mentioned it, but I'd seen that he was crying.

"Cross your heart," my brother told me.

I did so. I didn't wish for anything, want anything, say anything. I was in present time, standing in the muck, my shoes ruined, my skin itchy.

There was a log, no, a tree, the one hit by the same lightning that had struck the Dragon the second time around. An old moss-draped oak, dead now and pale, pale gray. Ice-colored in all this green, this muck, these leaves, this water, this heat. The Dragon walked toward it. He was knee-high in the water. He took off his undershirt and I saw the tree patterns the lightning had left on his arms and his torso. Like Lazarus. I felt a twinge of something sad. As if everything that was happening now had already happened, only to someone else.

The Dragon turned around and nodded. "Watch this."

He spit at the old log and there was a spark of fire. The Dragon waved his shirt around and smothered the flame, but the smoke had done what he'd expected. Dozens of bats rose from the log. They seemed pure black at first, but in the sunlight they shone, a glinty blue, then purple. It was like seeing the face of the world, like seeing every possibility there had ever been. Out of smoke, out of fire, out of wood, out of ice, they arose in a cloud.

Ned blinked. "Well, what do you know," he said.

"They're around all day long, only we never see them. You walk along and you think you're alone. But they're here," the Dragon said. "Along with all the other things we don't see."

The bats disappeared into the sky; from underneath they were gray-brown, like leaves falling upward, like time reversed.

My shoulders were sunburned, I could barely breathe in the heat, there was a tick walking along my shin, but it was worth it. If I hadn't learned my lesson, I would have wished we could stay there forever. But I knew better now. We'd seen what we'd come to see. The way to trick death. Breathe in. Breathe out. Watch as it all rises upward, black and blue into the even bluer sky.

I I

I CALLED FRANCES YORK TO APOLOGIZE FOR NEVER showing up for work. In my past life, before moving to Florida, I was the dependable one, the great co-worker, the planner of parties. As it was, I hadn't been to the library in a week. Hadn't called in once.

"Well, don't come in now," Frances told me. "Come to my house at six-thirty. Thirteen Palmetto Street. The house with the big yard."

"Look, if you want to fire me, I understand. You can do it over the phone. It's fine. I deserve it."

"I have never fired anyone in my life, and I am not about to start now. You're coming for dinner."

I didn't quite believe her. I dressed for the occasion of my firing. Somber. My hair combed back, a red headband that I'd picked up at the drugstore, and then, last-minute bribery, a plant from the florist. A Venus flytrap. Useful in Florida. Practical. The old me. The dependable girl. Maybe Frances would see she needed me, although the truth of it was, there was barely work enough for one of us at the library.

I'd never been to Frances's house; it was on the older side of town, where the yards were bigger and the feel was more rural, less suburban. Her house was old Florida, tin roof, shutters, cabbage palms. I parked and got out, carrying the potted plant, wearing good black shoes that were uncomfortable. I stopped on the path. There was something that looked like a bear on the front porch. It was growing dark and my vision wasn't great. I had a moment of panic. Then I realized it was the pup in her desk photos grown to a monstrous size. A Newfoundland. Not a breed that would do well in Florida, and as it was, I could hear the creature panting. When the creature woofed, Frances came out of the house. She was wearing blue jeans, an old shirt, a scarf around her head. She didn't resemble her library self.

"Quiet, Harry," she said to her dog. "Poor thing, some students got him, then realized they couldn't take care of him and left him behind when they went home for the summer. Happens every year. Abandonment."

"Good it wasn't a pony," I said.

When I approached, Harry sniffed me politely. He was slobbery, but gentlemanly. Not the pet I'd expected Frances to have.

"I thought you'd have a cat," I said. "The stereotype."

"Do you?"

"It's not officially mine. It belonged to a co-worker. It thinks it's mine when dinnertime comes around. And I had a mole. Adopted as well. I just released it into the wild. The hedge in front of my house, actually. I thought I'd better set it free before I killed it. I have terrible luck with living creatures."

"They came looking for Seth Jones," Frances said.

"What?" I couldn't have heard quite right. We were talking about pets, weren't we?

"Let's go in," Frances suggested.

I followed her, and the dog followed me. Had she said something about Seth Jones?

We sat down in the kitchen. Frances had made lemonade. Poured cherry juice into the pitcher, a faint blush, a sour pink. I could see it even though it was so pale. This was going to be worse than being fired. She wanted to talk about Lazarus, the man I never spoke about, the man I knew I would lose. Just not now. Not yet.

"The Orlon sheriff's office got a call from some character at a feedstore. That's how the whole thing started, and now they're convinced some crime has been committed. Nobody's seen this fellow Jones, not since he was struck by lightning, and now a deliveryman from the feedstore swears he recognized a man in Jones's house who wasn't Jones. It was someone who worked at the feedstore a while back. So now they're digging around." Frances let that all sink in, then she asked, "I suppose you want to know how I know all this."

"Yes, how?" I suppose I looked stunned. I certainly felt it.

"They came for his library information. His card."

Frances poured me a glass of lemonade.

"It was missing from the catalog, but I found it on your desk."

She knew a lot. More than I would have expected. She'd been seeing through me all along.

The dog was sitting beside me, hoping there'd be cookies to go with the lemonade, I suppose, breathing on my leg.

I thought about which sort of lie would fit best.

"Don't bother," Frances said before I could even begin. "I don't care how you're involved. We're going to burn the card, and just so they don't think we did so intentionally, we're going to burn all the others as well."

We went over to the pantry. The boxes of catalog cards had been stacked inside, including the ones from the basement. There was the musty, sad odor of paper. Frances had spent all week carrying boxes of cards home.

"Because what someone reads in a library is nobody else's business," Frances said.

We waited for the sun to go down. Then we dragged the boxes into the backyard, dumped some cards into the barbecue, then poured on some fire starter. It was pitch-black now, a hazy night. I had my backpack; I unzipped it and took out Seth Jones's cards. The ones I'd swiped.

"I appreciate your helping me," I said. "And just so you know, there hasn't been any criminal activity. Nothing like that."

"Don't tell me anything. I'm not helping you. It's something I believe in. Let them find their man some other way."

It took nearly three hours to burn all the cards. We drank all the lemonade, then switched to whiskey.

"The sheriff will be back tomorrow. I insisted I needed time to look up the gentleman in question's card. I'll let him know that over the years records have been lost."

I worried for Frances, putting herself on the line this way.

"Oh, I know our funds will be cut. If they close the library, people in town will have to go to the Hancock Public Library, or maybe the university will let them use their facility. Maybe I'll go to Paris. If I do, you can take care of Harry."

I laughed.

"I'm serious."

She just might be. We both had soot on our faces, under our nails, along with paper cuts from ripping up the catalog cards.

"He likes you," Frances said.

The dog was at my feet, a mountain of fur.

"I'm totally unlikable," I insisted.

The Newfie sighed and Frances and I both laughed.

We finished the whiskey, then had coffee to sober up. Now that we were done with the burning, we wet the ashes and scraped them into garbage bags, which I took with me when I left. No evidence. Harry followed me to my car and watched as I drove away. Nice dog, but I already had a pet.

I drove until I felt I'd found a safe place; I tossed the bag of ashes in the bin behind the diner. Then I headed out of town fast. I hadn't thought to phone Lazarus; I'd thought we had time. Now I wished I'd called him from Frances's house. I simply hadn't expected the authorities to move so quickly. When I got there I knew something was wrong before I turned into the driveway. I pulled over onto the shoulder of the road. From here I could see there were no longer any red oranges. Everything had turned black. Oranges were dropping from the trees, like stones. Through the trees, I saw the whirl of blue light.

There was a sheriff's car at the rise of the drive, so I kept going; I doubled around and drove back to the Interstate. By then, I was shaking. I wasn't sure if I'd done the right thing. Should I have driven right in and demanded to know what the hell was going on? Maybe I'd panicked. Or maybe I was smart. Either way, I was now on my way home. I stopped at the gas station in Lockhold and considered going back for Lazarus. I sat in my car for almost an hour, debating, and then I headed to Orlon.

I would hire a lawyer — that's what I'd do. I would stand beside him even if they thought he'd murdered Seth Jones. Perhaps I would be an accessory to murder in their eyes. Perhaps Lazarus wouldn't even be charged with anything. I stopped at another gas station. I didn't know if I should go backward or forward, so I just went nowhere. This time I got out and called the police station in Red Bank, New Jersey. It was a crazy thing to do and I wasn't sure why I did it. Some decisions you make and some seem to be made for you. I suppose I called the person I trusted most. The one whose opinion mattered. I stood near the restrooms in the dark, pushing quarters into the pay phone. Trucks rumbled by on the Interstate. When I got Jack Lyons on the phone he was quiet at first. He didn't seem to believe it was me.

"Of course it's me," I said. "The parking lot. You and me."

"Okay," he said. "You and me."

"I need to ask you some reference questions."

In our small town Jack had been in charge of death of all

sorts: homicide, suicide, double homicide, death by misad-
venture and by accidents, death by natural causes. When
folks saw him walk into the old-age home, the residents
crossed themselves, turned to look in the other direction,
knew one of them was gone for sure. When he went to talk
to the elementary-school kids about safety — no sticking
fingers into electrical outlets, no grabbing pots off the
stove — some of the children got hysterical and had to be
taken to the nurse's office. All that time Jack had been call-
ing me with reference questions, he could have looked up
the answers himself. I'd come to understand that. He knew
it all already, so maybe he simply liked my pronunciation of
asphyxiation, nightshade, West Nile virus.

Or maybe he just wanted to speak to me in my own
language.

"Where are you?" Jack asked. "You disappeared. I wrote
you a note, but you never wrote back."

"I moved to Florida. Better weather." What a joke. It was
about a hundred and five degrees and so humid my usually
straight-as-sticks hair had curled. The night smelled like
poison.

"I know you moved. You think I didn't take it upon my-
self to find out what had happened to you? I mean, where
are you right now? I hear traffic."

I thought about the way he used to look at me. He had
wanted something from me and he never got it. I thought
I'd been humiliating myself, but maybe I'd been doing the
very same thing to him. "I'm sorry, Jack."

"You're sorry that you disappeared and never bothered

to write? Or you're sorry that you never gave a shit about me and how I felt?"

"I didn't know what I wanted."

"As opposed to now."

I laughed. Maybe he did know me.

"So, what is it you want to talk about?" Jack went on. "Or let me guess. What did we always have in common? Oh, yeah. Death."

He sounded different, or maybe I'd never listened to him before. Maybe those times in his car and in the parking lot weren't exactly what I'd thought they were. Maybe he'd noticed the ice, the stones, the way I believed I deserved to be hurt.

"Are you making fun of me?" I wasn't used to feeling this way when I talked to him. It had been a long time, after all.

"Hey, baby, I am Mr. Death. Ask me your questions."

I'd called to ask him about Lazarus, about how I could help him if he was accused of murder. Should I help him flee, or tell him to stand up to everyone? But as it turned out, that's not what I really wanted to know.

I hesitated. That wasn't like me, I was overwhelmed with feeling.

"Go on. Shoot," Jack said. "Make it a good one. Give me a what-if."

So I did. I made it the only one.

"What if your brother is dying and you can't stop it. What do you do?"

All I could hear were the trucks. The gears grinding. So many people going somewhere. I was standing in a gas station in the middle of the night in Florida. It was as though I'd never talked to anyone before. I could hear Jack breathing. I wanted to cry. I'd never even really given him a chance. Dealing with so much death had given him the ability to find logic in an irrational world.

"You help him find something that makes him feel that he still wants to be alive. Only thing to do."

"Maybe you should have been the one at the reference desk."

I could have been anywhere on earth. I was that lost.

"Not me," Jack said. "It was always you."

WHEN I GOT HOME, I KNEW SOMEONE WAS THERE. GISELLE was on the lawn and I had left her inside. There was a spare key under my mailbox. Not very hard to find; when I slid my hand under the metal, it was no longer there. I crouched down beside the cat and rubbed under her chin and left her out a while longer. She didn't hate me as much, or maybe she'd grown used to me. Lazarus was asleep on the couch, one foot planted on the floor. He looked young, and tired, like a man who'd hitchhiked and walked all night. I locked all the doors, unplugged the phone. He had a duffel bag with him, which I took into the kitchen. You shouldn't do these things, I know, but I did it anyway. I unzipped the bag, looked through it. I suppose I was just making sure he was who I thought he was. There were some clothes, a wallet with a few hundred in cash, a plane ticket to Italy, a passport with Seth Jones's name and Lazarus's photo; at the very bottom I found the wooden box filled with ashes.

I replaced everything and put on some coffee. I got a new bag of coffee beans from the freezer, and I noticed the electricity must have gone out sometime during the night. My house was a mess. I'd paid no attention to it; but then, I'd never felt as though it belonged to me. I'd never really lived here. The closest thing to something familiar, something that belonged to me, were the few pieces of Renny's Doric temple still on the table. Giselle liked to play with the columns, batting them around until they fell on the floor.

I went to the back door to call her in now, but she wouldn't come. I had to go to her, out by the hedge. The sky was inky. The center of the horizon was the color of the bats I'd seen in pure daylight, deep blue, streaks of black and purple. When I bent down I saw that Giselle had gotten Renny's mole. I recognized it because of the bite out of its ear. We'd tried to save him and we couldn't. The little pet who had cheated death; it wasn't moving now.

"Bad girl," I scolded Giselle.

I sat cross-legged and picked up the mole and held him in the palm of my hand.

By the time Lazarus woke up I had buried the mole, made coffee, and telephoned my sister-in-law. My brother was still recovering from our trek to see the Dragon, but he was happy that we'd gone. Ever since, he'd been dreaming of bats and butterflies, Nina told me. He was writing a paper on chaos theory in fairy tales. He was writing like mad, up half the night. Things had become clear to him and he wanted to get it all down before it was too late. The tiniest action, the smallest creature, the most minute decision had huge ramifications. One mole dies, one is saved, only to die again. One word is spoken aloud and the world changes. An arm becomes a wing, a beast becomes a man, a girl is silent for a hundred years — frozen in place and in time — a young man has to search the world before he discovers who he really is.

I lay down beside Lazarus on the couch. His eyes opened. Ashes to ashes. They were so dark.

"Hey," he said to me. He was about to embrace me, kiss me, then he thought better of it. "I'll burn you."

I shook my head. I remembered what the Dragon had told us about fire. I handed Lazarus two cloves of garlic that I'd peeled in the kitchen. "The remedy," I told him.

Another man might have questioned me, might have failed the test. Lazarus looked at me, then ate the garlic. I put my head against his chest. I didn't feel the same heat from inside him.

Lazarus had seen the delivery truck from his window and he'd also recognized the driver, Hal Evans. He knew him because they'd had an altercation when they were working together at the feedstore. Hal had come in drunk and had been saying this and that, goading Lazarus. Lazarus had left some bags of fertilizer in the other man's path and Hal had stumbled. Hal Evans was the worst of all people to come sniffing around the orchard. Maybe he'd heard the rumors the farmworkers had spread, that they worked for a monster, a man who refused to be seen, that there was something not right in the house where all the window shades were drawn.

Lazarus packed a bag as soon as Hal's truck pulled out. He'd been waiting for something like this for a while; now he waited for what came next. Later that day, someone he didn't recognize was talking to the workers in the field. He saw them looking at the house, conversing with the men he employed. That afternoon he walked out the back door. He figured any phone calls he made would be traced, but walking, he knew what that did: it made you a free man.

Lazarus was shivering, so I covered him with a blanket. The morning was bright. We blinked in the light of it. I told myself not to make a wish, or if I did, if I had to, if I just couldn't stop myself, then to make one for him. Lazarus fell back asleep; he was exhausted and couldn't wake up. I wanted to let him dream for as long as he could. He had walked for miles. I looked at him. I could taste the garlic, the cure, the end of everything, the beginning of everything.

I got dressed and went to the bank. Peggy, my physical therapist, was there on line and she congratulated me on how good I looked. "You worked hard," she said to me. "The comeback kid."

Had I? I suppose I had. Those exercises that made me want to cry, dragging my left side along. It felt almost normal now, only not quite; there was still a metallic feeling along my ribs, around my heart. You couldn't see it, but it was there, just as surely as Renny's hands were filled with strands of gold.

I withdrew everything in my account except for a hundred dollars.

"Big purchase?" the teller asked me. Everybody knew everybody in this town. Even me.

I smiled. Very big. I said I wanted cash because I was buying a used car. An old Corvette.

"I'm jealous," the teller said.

I had fifteen thousand dollars left from the sale of my grandmother's house, but it fit neatly in my backpack.

"It's red," I said.

"The best," the teller said to me.

I walked to the parking lot. There was my Honda. The one with the good tires, the safe tires my brother had chosen before we left New Jersey. When I got home, Lazarus was still asleep. I understood. He didn't want to wake up. I sat in a chair. Maybe I cried. I loved him in a way that was over. A way that was the beginning of something. The sort of love that opened you up for more.

When it was late afternoon I got onto the couch beside him. I whispered that it was time for him to go.

I won't, he said.

You will, I thought. *You want to.*

This would be the moment I would never let go of, even though it caused me the greatest pain. When I was old, when I couldn't walk or talk or see, I would still have this.

He assumed I was going with him. We'd leave the cat outside and someone would find her, care for her. Wasn't that the way it went? Cats made their own homes, found their own way. I could send my brother a note, mail it from the road, not until we got where we were going, all those places, Venice and Paris, everywhere I'd ever wanted to go.

He packed the cash into his duffel bag. I watched his hands. I couldn't look at anything else.

This was what it was. The ruin of it. The depth of it. Have it once and you can have it again. That's the riddle. That's the truth.

* * *

Lazarus took a shower, drank iced coffee, had a bowl of cold tomato soup. It was humid outside and when the day was over, the night was sticky hot. It was late when we left and the sky was dark. We drove to Jacksonville, on the side roads. I knew the way there. A place where no one would recognize us. We drove for an hour, then two. It seemed that we were going somewhere together. His hand on me as I drove. I could feel him, but it wasn't enough. He should have known I wasn't going with him: he should have noticed I left the cat in the house, something I would have never done if I hadn't been coming back. I wasn't somebody who left that way.

I took him to the bus station. All he needed to do was find someone who could change the date of birth on his passport and then he'd be Seth Jones. But for now, he needed to get out of Florida. I bought one ticket for the next bus; it was headed to Atlanta.

We sat at the bus station together till five in the morning. That was when the bus was leaving. And here's the thing: We didn't look at each other. We didn't beg each other for anything. We'd already given each other all that we had.

"So, this is the way it ends," he said.

People around us were sleeping. They had their own stories; they weren't listening to us. There was a child in a red sweater in her mother's arms. There was the sun through the dirty foggy window.

Not at all, I thought. *This is the way it begins.*

Brother and Sister

I

W E KNEW IT WAS GETTING CLOSER BECAUSE
my brother was dreaming of butterflies. Even in
the daytime, he was dreaming. At first the mete-
orology society had refused to accept his paper,
"Chaos Theory and Fairy Tales." I had to stay
with Ned overnight while Nina flew up to speak
to the head of the society. When she came back
she reported that the decision had been changed.

By the time Ned went to Washington DC to
deliver his paper, he was in a wheelchair; the

moderator had to lower the microphone and ask for complete silence so that Ned's reedy voice could be heard. At the heart of his paper was the notion that fairy tales relieved us of our need for order and allowed us impossible, irrational desires. Magic was real, that was his thesis. This thesis was at the very center of chaos theory — if the tiniest of actions reverberated throughout the universe in invisible and unexpected ways, changing the weather and the climate, then anything was possible. The girl who sleeps for a hundred years does so because of a single choice to thread a needle. The golden ball that falls down the well rattles the world, changing everything. The bird that drops a feather, the butterfly that moves its wings, all of it drifts across the universe, through the woods, to the other side of the mountain. The dust you breathe in was once breathed out. The person you are, the weather around you, all of it a spell you can't understand or explain.

He got a standing ovation, Nina told me. We were setting up the nursery together now that they were back from DC, painting a watercolor mural on the wall. Nina was supposed to take it easy — she had preeclampsia, high blood pressure brought on by pregnancy — but she painted flowers and trees in the baby's room after she came home from classes. Sometimes Ned would watch us, and then we'd turn around, ready to joke with him, and he'd be asleep. We kept painting. Nina was at work on the sun. My job was the moon.

Sometimes my brother cried out in his sleep, sometimes he called out.

"Butterflies," Nina said. "In his dreams."

Nina had dark circles under her eyes. Now, when my

brother went to all his medical appointments, they let him have whatever he needed to kill the pain. That should be a good thing, but it's not, because then you know you're nearing the end.

I offered to help out full-time, and Nina let me. They had closed the library, just as Frances had suspected. I had no job and was collecting unemployment benefits. I didn't think about what I would do when my money ran out. I could always get a job as a cashier at Acres' Hardware. People would still ask me questions there. Reference me a saw, a hammer, a can of paint, an apron, an anvil. I would learn it all, recite it by heart.

But for now, I was available. I did the food shopping and the laundry. I felt useful for once. I began to paint butterflies on the wall. I began to dream of them, too. I thought of Lazarus, surely halfway across the world by now. I dreamed of him as well, but only occasionally. I was too busy for that now.

My brother had started to age, the way ill people do. He was a hundred years old when he slept in his wheelchair; he was breaking our hearts. When he napped, Nina and I sat out on the grass, even when it was hot. There was a hedge of boxwood. We sat in its shade. Nina cried; I watched her. Once, I went into the kitchen to fetch some ice water for Nina and found my brother at the window.

"Do you think we all have something we dream of doing?" my brother said. At that moment he was perfectly alert.

I sat down at the table. "Such as?"

"The thousands of monarch butterflies. In migration. The thousands of changes. All chaos. All one moment. That's what I've always wanted to see. I want to see that."

He sounded upset. I'd never heard my brother want something quite so deeply, so much. This was far beyond his desire to see the old man in Jacksonville. That was a lark; this was the heart of the matter. The end of his life.

We hadn't heard, but Nina had come in, looking for me. She was still crying, but she looked like stone, the way she had when I spied her in the yard. There were bits of grass on her clothes. She smelled like boxwood and evergreen. She was stronger than you'd think. She simply didn't give away who she was to just anyone. She probably started to plan it out then. When she heard his dream.

A nurse came in once a week while I went with Nina to her Lamaze classes at the health center at the university. The other women were younger, graduate students, wives of young professors, two lesbian couples. Everyone seemed so sure of the future. They had potluck dinners together on the weekends. We never went to those. Maybe everyone thought Nina and I were a couple. I suppose for those hours of class we were.

"She's the best breather in the class," I told Ned.

"Of course. Naturally." He was proud of her. He was in love with her. But he was also in the process of leaving. He often sat at the window and stared at the yard and I wasn't quite certain he was seeing what we were seeing.

I did get a card from Seth Jones. The postmark was Florence, so he'd made it there. He wrote, *Plan to take the ashes to Venice. Wish you were here. SJ.*

I didn't. I wanted to be exactly where I was, sitting with my brother in the afternoons, fixing dinner and washing up afterward, playing cards with Nina in the evenings. One day a package arrived for my brother; it was a bathrobe, sent by Jack Lyons.

"Who the hell is Jack Lyons?" Ned asked. He liked the bathrobe but felt odd accepting a gift from a stranger.

"You went to high school with him in Red Bank. And I used to sleep with him."

"He has good taste," Ned said.

"Shut up."

"I meant in bathrobes."

Jack knew what the dying needed. He was far more of an expert than I'd ever been. Even when I didn't contact him, he continued to send my brother gifts. As for Ned, he'd started to wait for the packages. Look forward to them. One week there was a tape of birdcalls that my brother liked to have played while he napped. Another time there were two pairs of heavy woolen socks. And then came a huge box of fudge, the old-fashioned kind. My brother couldn't eat it, but he loved the smell.

At last I called New Jersey. "You don't have to send my brother anything," I told Jack.

"I don't need you to tell me what to do," he said back.

There wasn't much of an answer for that.

"He loves the birdsong tape. And the fudge."

I was glad it was impossible for Jack to see me. I was in sweatpants and a T-shirt, Giselle curled on my lap. I had all the lights turned off to cut down on my electricity bills. I had recently applied for a job at Acres' Hardware Store, only to be told I was unqualified.

I had my hand over the phone receiver. I was crying.

"I know what you're doing," Jack said.

"You're such an expert." I sounded snotty and bitter and desperate.

"About some things. Most people cry for good reason. Most people smile for good reasons, too."

The next package he sent contained wind chimes. My brother had us put them up by the window. He smiled whenever he heard them. It was a gift for my brother, but it was also a message to me. There was something still worth having in his world.

"Did I know this guy Jack?" Ned asked. He was at the point of repeating all of our conversations. His memory was gone, and the here and now was going as well.

"No," I said. "Nobody did."

"He has good taste."

"Seems to," I had to agree.

At night, when Nina was exhausted, I sat with my brother and read him fairy tales.

"Read the one I like," he said one night.

"It's not in this collection," I lied.

"Liar."

But I would not read the story about death, not now, not when we knew what the ending was. I read "Hansel and Gretel" and "The Juniper Tree" and "Brother and Sister"; I read about fishermen's wives and horses that were loyal, and then I told him the story I'd made up, about the frozen girl on the mountain.

"Now that's a sad one," my brother said. "All she has to do is pick up her feet and walk away and she won't turn to ice. Even when we were kids and you told me, I never understood that girl."

I wanted to change what was happening, but it couldn't be done. I bit my tongue a thousand times a day. I wasn't about to wish for anything. I was afraid of wishes still. But Nina wasn't. She had gone to her doctor, who said she could no longer travel. My brother had made it to sixth months. He loved to put his hand on Nina and feel the baby moving. Nina didn't tell me, but she bought the tickets for his dream. She started to teach me how to give Ned his injections of antibiotics and Demerol. She taught me how to work the IV when he needed more fluid.

"What's the best way to die?" I asked Jack one night. I usually called him at work, but this time I'd phoned him at home. He still seemed surprised to hear from me, but he answered me right away.

"Living," he said. He didn't even have to think about it. It was as if he'd always known the answer.

When Nina told me she wanted me to take Ned to California most of what I felt was terror. Her doctor had told her she couldn't make the trip because of her condition. But surely I wasn't up to the task. I wasn't up to anything. My brother was leaving so fast. He was in diapers now. He was going backward in time. Every time he woke up he talked about the butterflies. Once in his life, that's what he wanted; well, this was that once. Nina had called a friend in Monterey who would pick us up at the airport in San Francisco; Eliza, a nurse, would come with a rented ambulance and take us to her house. The migration was already happening, she'd told Nina. Eliza's husband, Carlos, would take us to Big Sur, where the monarchs spend the winter. We would get there by ambulance if necessary.

"It's too much for him," I said.

"It's not enough," Nina told me.

She had that stony look. She was the woman who'd been reading about the hundred ways to die. She wanted my brother to have everything he'd ever wanted.

I packed a bag that night. A carry-on, since the suitcase would be filled with medicine. Nina hired a medevac plane. She had already taken a second mortgage on the house. If she never had another car, if she and the baby had to walk everywhere, eat rice, read by candlelight, she still wanted this. Even if she couldn't be there.

"You're going to see the butterflies," she said to my brother on the morning it was to happen.

"No." He smiled at her. He didn't believe it. He was still traveling backward through time. Younger than he had been on the night my mother died. I was the older sister now. I was the hand to hold.

"I can't go, because of the baby, but your sister's going to take you to California."

"What do you know?" My brother closed his eyes, exhausted just thinking about it.

"I know I love you," Nina said.

She was kneeling beside his bed. I had never witnessed such an act of generosity. Ned had on both pairs of socks Jack had sent. There were the wind chimes swinging back and forth in the window. I had been wrong about everything. I was terrified to go.

"Don't worry," Nina said. We had to take him to the airport by ambulance — how could I not be worried? "You'll manage."

At least her friend Eliza was a nurse. I wouldn't be all alone in this.

"Are you sure you want to go ahead? You probably won't be with him when it happens." *When he goes,* I meant to say. But I couldn't.

Nina put her arms around me. She told me a secret. "I will be," she said.

We gave my brother his maximum amount of Demerol and got on the plane. There were two EMTs with us, so I slept for a while. When I woke I felt weightless. There were clouds all around us. My brother was hooked up to an IV and the machine made a clicking noise. I realized the clicking inside my head had disappeared some time ago and I hadn't even noticed. I could see Ned's feet, the socks Jack had sent him. I might have sobbed. One of the EMTs, a man about my age, sat down across from me and took my hand.

Over the Rockies, my brother was in pain. The sky was the brightest blue I'd ever seen, dotted with puffballs. I wondered if this was what the sky was like in Italy. So blue. So open. We were floating through space and time. But I didn't wish we would always be there. I knew this was only an instant. I gave Ned one of his injections, to make sure I was capable, with the experts looking on.

"There you go," the EMT said. "Just like an old pro."

I didn't want to get to know him, or the other one, the young woman. I didn't have any space for anything more than I was already carrying. I described the clouds to my brother.

"Cumulus," he said.

His mouth was dry, so the woman EMT traveling with us gave him ice to suck on.

"Ice," he said. "Very nice. Unless it's on the porch."

Ned and I laughed.

"Private joke," I told the EMTs.

Ned was asleep when we landed at San Francisco. The ambulance was parked on the runway and Nina's friend Eliza was there. She and Nina had grown up next door to each other in Menlo Park, and she was Nina's opposite, dark and jovial, even now when Ned cried in pain as he was being transferred.

"We'll have him in a nice big bed soon," Eliza reassured me. "We'll take good care of you," she told my brother.

Eliza telephoned Nina from the runway and then held the phone up to Ned's ear. He smiled when he heard his wife's voice. I don't know what Nina said to him, but she comforted him somehow, and he slept all the way to Eliza's house in Monterey, a long trip, so tiresome I fell asleep myself, sitting up, my check against the window.

When I opened my eyes all I saw was green. And then the sky, and then the clouds.

"Almost there," Eliza said cheerfully.

The ambulance pulled up in her driveway. I sat beside Ned while they got the stretcher ready. I could see Eliza's husband come out to meet the EMTs. New ones now. The ones from the plane had disappeared.

"My fucking back," Ned said. "It hurts."

"Serves you right for being such a pain in the ass."

A joke from a thousand years ago. He remembered.

"You're the pain. You."

*   *   *

I THINK NED TOOK THE DISHES OFF THE TABLE WHEN HE found them there that morning. I think he put them in the sink when he realized what it meant for our mother to have left breakfast for us. He did the logical thing in an illogical world. He cleaned up the mess.

I hopped out of the ambulance so Carlos and the EMTs could carry Ned inside. It was beautiful here, wherever we were. I blinked. A bat. There beyond the trees.

"Go to sleep," Eliza told me. "We'll wake you in a few hours, and then we'd better go right there."

She was a nurse. She saw where my brother was. That he was leaving right now.

"I don't need to sleep," I said.

"An hour," Eliza insisted. "Then we'll be ready to go."

They had a pullout couch made up for me. They were kind, and I accepted their kindness, even though I knew I'd never see them again, never be able to repay them.

When I woke up I could hear my brother and Eliza talking. She asked him if he wanted food, applesauce, or homemade vanilla pudding, or crackers softened in water.

"Nope," my brother said. "I couldn't stomach it. That's a joke. Get it?"

I heard Eliza's laughter. I got up, found the bathroom, washed my face. Today was the day. It was the start of the *ever after*. I ran a stranger's brush through my hair. It was longer than it had been since I was eight years old. Black. Sticks. Crow-colored.

I went into the guest room. My brother looked happy. He looked like a cloud.

"Guess where we are," he said.

"The middle of your dream?"

"Monterey, California," my brother said.

He was still here. Right here with me. And I was grateful for that.

Carlos and Eliza took him out to their van, and rested him in the back. An ambulance might not want to go as far into the forest as we meant to go. I got in the front seat while Eliza hooked up Ned's IV and gave him all his meds. It was another ride, but it wouldn't be as long. Carlos got behind the wheel. He worked for the parks department.

"We try to keep this week secret," he said. "So we don't have tourists up the ying-yang. Plus we never know exactly. All fall they arrive in dribs and drabs and then all at once. They're everywhere. That's why it was all so spur-of-the-moment. But you made it in time, Ned," he called to my brother.

It didn't take that long to get there, but the road was curvy. It was the most beautiful place I had ever been. "Can you see out there?" I called to Ned.

Lying on his back, he could see the sky.

"Cirrus," he called back.

His voice was a hundred years old. But he sounded happy. When I walked into the kitchen all those years ago, Ned was tossing something into the trash; he was piling the dishes into the sink. Our mother had left us two bowls of cereal, two glasses of juice, our vitamin pills, the sugar bowl, two spoons, blueberry muffins, cut in half.

My eyes were filled with sleep when I walked into the kitchen that morning. My brother had looked guilty because he knew something I didn't know. He looked ashamed, as though he had a secret that was too bad to share.

It's too early. Go back to bed.

Beautiful long, stretched-out clouds drifted all along the ocean. Big black rocks. The curving road. The smell of something. I stuck my head out the window, breathed deep. *The here* and *the now* of it blew me away. But I didn't wish for anything. Not more. Not less. I was exactly where I was, head hanging out the window, feeling the wind, tears in my eyes. The scent of this place was amazing.

"Eucalyptus," Carlos said. "It's what attracts the butterflies. The groves."

I had no sense of what time it was. I think we had traveled through a day and a night. It was still morning, Eliza told me. I felt more for her than I had for people I'd known for years.

"He's holding up," she said, but the way she said it made me know, not for long.

We pulled into a parking lot. There was the Santa Lucia Range in front of us. And nearer, Mt. Lion. All rocks and trees. The ocean was so blue I couldn't believe it. We were in a picnic area, but it was early and the lot was empty. Luck for once. Pure luck.

"We've got it all to ourselves," Carlos said. "And a day without fog. That's a miracle."

The three of us got Ned onto the stretcher, into the fresh air. I carried the IV pole.

"Green," Ned said.

It was. It was a eucalyptus grove. So delicious. Like the world was brand-new. We went up a path, slowly; pine needles make you slip, so carefully, carefully. The air was cold and warm at the same time — cool in the shadows, lemony in the sun. We crested a ridge. I thought there were falling leaves at first. All those orange things. Everywhere.

But no.

I leaned down and whispered to my brother, "You won't believe this."

We went into the sunlight and they were everywhere. In front of us were several picnic tables made of redwood, and we hauled the stretcher up on one. Settled it down, slowly.

"My, my, my," my brother said.

There was a whirlwind of monarchs. You could hear the beating of their wings. I stood there with my arms out and they lit upon me, everywhere; they hung on my fingers, walked in my hair.

Carlos and Eliza were standing on a picnic bench, arms around each other.

"More," they both said, and they laughed and drew each other near so that the butterflies swirled between them.

There were too many to count, everywhere, thousands of them, sleepy, slow, whirling. It was the height of their migration, and they were exhausted and beautiful. So orange they were like rubies, red, red, red.

I borrowed Eliza's cell phone. The service was bad, but when I put the phone up to my brother's ear he could hear Nina. He knew it was her.

"Everything has just changed a thousand times over."

It took all of his effort to say that. When he had, we turned off the phone and waited. I had the desperate urge to turn my brother around. *Quick,* I would say, *we have to do it now. Put your feet where your head is resting. Play the final trick. Let Death pass over; let it pass by. Please, let us try.* But I didn't say that. I didn't say anything.

Eliza unhooked the IV right before it happened. There was a click, and then quiet. You wouldn't think there could be so many butterflies in the world. You wouldn't think everything could change in an instant. But there are, and it does.

There were whirling clouds above us, brought in from the cold ocean air. Nimbus. Fast moving. Flying. Good to lift your spirit. Good for everything. Good for him.

II

NINA NAMED THEIR DAUGHTER MARIPOSA. SHE WAS born in January on a day when there wasn't a cloud in the sky. I noticed. I was keeping track of such things. I was there with Mariposa when she was born; I was the coach who said, *Breathe* and *Push* and *Oh my God, there has never been anything so beautiful.* I was watching over her from the beginning, so I was made her godmother, which meant I had to watch over her forever more. It turned out to be something I was good at. Something I was meant to be. I stayed on for several months, babysitting, helping out, nearly learning to cook, until Nina was ready to go back to work, ready to have her daughter go to the day care center at the university while she taught her classes. I left Giselle with them. It just made sense. She was a Florida cat now. She'd have howled if she'd been made to put a paw into snow and ice. Besides, I'd never thought she was mine, so I wasn't really giving anything away.

A godmother's role is to send gifts, and I do that — too much, probably. Every year on Mariposa's birthday, I go for a visit. I don't despair over that time of the year anymore. It's my favorite month, just as it used to be. I've given Mariposa a dozen volumes of fairy tales. Her favorites are the Andrew Lang books, with all those pretty covers, filled with stories that feel illogical and true at the very same time. She and I are both partial to the Red Book.

Once I read Mari her father's favorite, "Godfather Death." "That's not funny," she said to me.

"No, it's not," I agreed. "But your father liked that story. He was a scientist like the doctor."

"They don't all have to be funny," she said after thinking it over. "But tell me the one about a girl who climbs a mountain that no one has ever climbed before."

"I don't know that one. I only know the one about the girl who was turned into ice."

"Make it up." Mariposa had a solemn face that reminded me of Ned. Ned, who was a good secret-keeper. Ned, who never believed in perfect logic. Ned, in the *ever after*.

It was difficult for me to say no to Mariposa. I wanted her to have everything. So I made up the story for her. It turned out to be a good one. Better than the story I used to tell myself. It was the same girl, in the same icy land, but this time she thought to climb over the mountain instead of standing in place and freezing. She was smarter now, less likely to

give in. As soon as she got to the place on the other side of
the mountain, she started to melt; she left a blue river behind
her, one that is always cold, always pure, always true.

The last time I visited Orlon, I took Mariposa out to
the orange grove. I was babysitting. Nina was at class, and
Mariposa had turned six. That's the way it happened. Time
kept moving forward. We sang songs as we drove, ones
I thought I would have forgotten by now. Mariposa made
me remember things. She liked my horrible voice and ap-
plauded. Everything she did was a treasure in my eyes. I was
the godmother, after all. She belonged to me, too.

When we got to the orchard I pulled into the driveway,
parked, and took Mari for a walk. She wore her hair in a
pixie cut. Nina had told me she refused to let her hair grow;
she hated to have it brushed and braided and fooled with.

"Smart girl," I said. I told her that a lot.

"It smells good here," Mari said as we walked in the grove.

She was right about that, too. The land had been sold at
auction, and all the trees were in bloom. We walked down
the road and waved to some of the workers.

"Hello!" Mariposa called to one of them who was pruning
the branches. "Do you live in a tree?"

I have thought of Lazarus Jones, but he's like a story I
heard long ago. A story where I turned the pages even
though I knew how it would end. Some things are like that,
chaos theory aside. Turn left or turn right, you come to the
same conclusions about certain things, the very same results.
A young man who was in the wrong place at the wrong
time, who wasn't afraid of death, who, when he got a chance
to be someone else, had to take it.

By now the hole in the ground had been filled in with stone and rock. I suppose the new owner hoped to cover it with fertilizer and sod, maybe reclaim the soil. All the old trees had been cut down. I thought I saw a red orange on one of the trees, but it was just the slant of sunlight, turning a piece of orange fruit crimson.

My mother's secret was that she never planned to meet her friends. The riddle of who she was. It was her thirtieth birthday. It was her least favorite month of the year. I had always liked January. I liked ice. It was beautiful, like diamonds, the brightest thing in the world. I liked to write my name in the cold, foggy window of my bedroom with my fingertip. I liked how black the sky was, how the stars seemed to hang down lower in the sky. It was before I cut off all my hair, froze my heart, blamed myself for everything that had ever happened. I was thinking about the future back then. I was looking forward.

My mother had something else in mind. Ned didn't want me to know, so he hid the dishes she'd set out before she got in her car. He hid the fact that our mother hadn't intended to come back. But maybe I knew anyway. Maybe I saw it on her face, in the sadness of the days before her birthday. I had caught her crying in the bathroom on more than one occasion. Our mother was the sort of person who didn't do well alone, and even though she was with us, she was alone. She'd never heard the story of the girl who climbed up the mountain no one had ever climbed before. I hadn't thought it up yet. She didn't have any wishes left, or at least that's what she must have believed, so the idea of a birthday might have stopped her cold. Nothing had turned out right. Except

maybe us, maybe that's why she left us breakfast, so we
wouldn't be worried and hungry. She probably didn't even
consider the way we would miss her. Each and every minute
of each and every day.

I wondered if my mother's last thoughts had been of us.
Her children, home and safe. If her heart broke, it wasn't
because of the ice but because of us. Good-bye to us. Me on
the porch, my brother at the window, the bats in the eaves of
the roof. Good-bye. Good-bye. This last moment, that last
moment. The ever after. The swirl of the sky.

If someone had told me of her plan, I could have chased
after the car for miles. But it wouldn't have mattered. She
had already decided. She took one last moment of care to
make certain we wouldn't be hungry when we woke. When
she saw the ice she probably felt she was lucky. Maybe that
was her final wish. Some luck for once in her life. The life
she'd had enough of. When she leaned down to kiss me
good-bye maybe I heard it in her voice. She said, *Good-bye,
my darling girl.* It may have been easier to blame myself than
to think she would leave us that way. If she came back now, I
do think she would know me; she'd still recognize me.

I have become the head of the reference desk in the library
in Red Bank. Back where I used to be. A citizen of New Jer-
sey. I never miss a day of work, and I'm a careful driver. I do
check my tires in the fall, so they'll be ready for the winter to
come. I have now counted thirty-two colors of ice, from in-
digo to scarlet. Maybe it's the chemicals they use to salt the
road, maybe it's the way the light filters through the bare
trees, maybe I'm just more sensitive to color than most
people. In our house, every room is red, each a different

shade: ruby, scarlet, cherry. Some people think it's all the same, but the tones couldn't be more different, as much so as black from white. Jack says I see what I want to see and hear what I want to hear and he wouldn't have it any other way. *Paint the ceiling red, if that's the way you want it.* He'll be surprised when and if I do. He doesn't seem to mind surprises. One time, when I drove back from Florida I had the Newfoundland, Harry, in the car. Frances had retired, off to France as she'd planned, and I was always one to adopt a pet.

"Did you meet a bear on the road?" Jack asked me when I let Harry out of the car.

"I met you," I said.

"You're trying to flatter me so I don't see how huge that dog is." Jack had laughed. "He'll take up half the living room."

And that was the end of the conversation. Jack just whistled for the dog. He had faith in me and in my choices. We left it at that.

This is what I know, the one and only thing. The best way to die is while you're living, even here in New Jersey. Even for someone like me. You'd laugh to know how long it's taken me to figure that out, when all I had to do was cross over the mountains. When I walk to my car in the parking lot on winter nights, I have often noticed bats, a black cloud in the darkening sky. They bring me comfort. They make me feel you're not so far away. To think, I used to be afraid. I used to run and hide. Now I stand and look upward. I don't mind what the weather is; the cold has never bothered me. I hope what I'm seeing is the ever after. I hope it's you.

Reading Group Guide

THE ICE QUEEN

A novel by

Alice Hoffman

A Conversation with

ALICE HOFFMAN

The author of *The Ice Queen* talks with Ellen Kanner of the *Miami Herald*

Ice and its opposite figure prominently in Alice Hoffman's new novel, *The Ice Queen,* but though the author writes richly about the natural world — the world we can see — she also writes about the supernatural, the world beyond our sight, where breath can boil water.

Hoffman believes in magic, even if we don't. The magic in her seventeen novels is not the David Blaine variety but the sort that is even harder to grasp — the magic we miss in our everyday lives. We don't see it because the enchantment is often of our own making, in the choices or the wishes we make. "I made my wish in January, the season of ice," says Hoffman's unnamed narrator and, in doing so, seals her fate.

The author, who lives outside Boston, made her debut in 1977 with *Property Of* at age twenty-five. She has since written an impressive array of bestsellers, including *Turtle Moon, Practical Magic,* and *Here on Earth,* plus half a dozen books for young readers.

Florida is featured in several of your works, including The Ice Queen, *with unlovely-sounding Orlon, Florida, lightning capital of the world. What's your relationship with Florida, and what do we need to do to redeem ourselves?*

I love Florida. I used to go with my mother in the winter when I was a kid. I wish I had grown up there. I feel like I'm a little in love with Florida's landscape. It was a dream place, the only kind of bright spot in our lives. I have memories of going to Parrot Jungle, to Monkey Jungle, the pre–Disney World theme parks. Those memories of youth seem more real than my everyday life.

The narrator of The Ice Queen *talks about the differences between Hans Christian Andersen and the Brothers Grimm. She prefers Grimm tales. So do you. Why?*

I always felt Andersen stories were really preachy, about being good and toeing the line. Grimm is the opposite. They go to some deep part you're afraid to go to, like pushing the witch into the oven. They're a way of dealing with what's scary but removed, so you don't feel like it's happening in your house. What fairy tales do is tell you the underneath of stories in psychological symbolism. They're what you really feel, the deepest darkest feelings. Kids have those feelings, too, and to pretend they don't seems so dishonest.

How does writing for children differ from writing for adults?

When I write for teens, I censor less. I get to a deeper, rawer place. I think they're willing to accept that. I wrote *Green Angel* after 9/11. I couldn't have written an adult book about 9/11. I wrote it for teenagers, for the sixteen-year-old girl I was, for what I used to know. I felt freer in a way. My new book, *The Foretelling,* is really different for me, about an Amazon girl in the Bronze Age. . . . I just channel her.

How was writing Moondog *with your son?*

I did it when he was ten and I had cancer; I was really sick when we did it. I wanted him to know what I did. It was a very long process — a picture book can take six years — but it was fun.

What was the catalyst for The Ice Queen?

I'm interested in the weather, the landscape. What recently happened with the tsunami in Southeast Asia is so nightmarish. Everybody's going about their daily life, and then you realize how tiny you are and how little you can control things.

I usually don't know where a book is coming from till it's over. Then it reveals itself to me. To be honest, when I think of it now, I'm thinking *The Ice Queen* is about being a survivor. I'm a cancer survivor; the narrator of *The Ice Queen* was hit right where I was hit; so I guess I'm writing about how to survive your life.

You've reflected on the death of many people you loved, your own breast cancer, 9/11, and a tsunami. What's still magical to you?

Writing. The weird thing is I'm really analytical, extremely analytical, but the writer in me isn't that way. It's like taking a drug or absinthe. That's the appeal for me. That's why I write so much. It's the dream that goes where the real you wouldn't go.

The complete text of Ellen Kanner's conversation with Alice originally appeared in the *Miami Herald* on April 24, 2005. Reprinted with permission.

QUESTIONS AND TOPICS FOR DISCUSSION

1. *The Ice Queen* begins with a warning: "Be careful what you wish for. . . . Wishes are brutal, unforgiving things." Considering the power of wishes as depicted in the novel, do you agree with the narrator's advice?

2. The narrator and her brother react quite differently to the news of their mother's death. Discuss how their differing responses reflect their individual characters. When the narrator discovers the truth about her mother's departure on the night she died, how does this news affect her?

3. The lines between life and death are unmistakably blurred in *The Ice Queen*. Some characters cheat death while others have difficulty embracing life. How do you think the narrator views her own mortality? In your opinion, has she cheated death?

4. Discuss the role of fairy tales in *The Ice Queen*. What kinds of tales does the narrator express a preference for? Why?

5. The physical effects of a lightning strike are unique to each victim in the novel — the narrator's inability to see red, Lazarus's boiling breath, Renny's hands, the Dragon's fire, and the Naked Man's sleepiness. Discuss the significance of some of these physical changes.

6. The author writes that "the elements most drawn to each other are the ones that destroy each other" (page 85). How does this theory play out in her relationship with Lazarus?

7. The old man known as the Dragon is an almost mythic character in the book. What realizations do the narrator and her brother draw from their pivotal encounter with him?

8. Early in the novel, the narrator admits her fascination with death. Yet she notes that she "didn't like stories in which Death was a major character" (page 43). Why does she draw this distinction? What does it reveal about her?

9. The narrator's two romantic interests, Lazarus and Jack, are very different from each other. What does each of these men offer her? Do you agree with the narrator's choice in the end? Why or why not?

10. In *The Ice Queen,* emotional scars can run far deeper than physical scars. Have the narrator's scars truly healed? Why is the new loss she experiences at the end of the book not as devastating as the loss of her mother?

11. Why do you think the author chose not to reveal the name of the narrator of *The Ice Queen*?